Nothing Brave Here

D1563345

Nothing Brave Here

short stories

JOAN CENEDELLA

For Pearl —
So *good* to see
you — Happy Reading —
love
Joan

Gallery of Readers Press

2013

This book was designed and typeset by Stephanie Gibbs;
printed and bound at Bridgeport National Bindery, Agawam,
Massachusetts.

Gallery of Readers Press
Carol Edelstein & Robin Barber, Publishers
16 Vernon Street
Northampton, Massachusetts 01060
www.galleryofreaders.org

ISBN 9780982944875

For Fran

Table of Contents

Big

The young boy saw the dog at the end of its leash and began to run toward the water, his progress impaired by the banging and rubbing of his inner thighs against each other, the lumbering of his butt from side to side. He looked like a tiny fat man with a child's face. The layer of smooth, tight blubber over his arms, chest and neck seemed to be choking him. As he labored across the beach toward his mother, his stubby arms flailing, he turned back again and again, his mouth open in alarm, to judge the distance between himself and the dog. His mother, standing at the edge of the water, looked at him and laughed her harsh laugh.

"There ain't nothin' to be afraid of, a dog on a leash, you dummy," she shouted out. Everyone, all the other kids and their mothers heard her, and he saw himself as if looking from a distance, a fat kid, a scaredy-cat, clumsy, running to his mother.

He blundered forward, but past her into the lake, heaved himself with a great splash onto a floating rubber tube. He laughed as if he didn't care, laughed himself into a frenzy, beating and pounding the rubber tube.

Harvey sighed. It was a dream, a movie, this earliest memory, coming on him sometimes in the morning as he woke up and sometimes, like now, during the day, out of nowhere. He wished it would leave him alone. It was his earliest memory, his beginning. At home his mother had stuffed him full of food, eating almost nothing herself. He didn't remember any father. It was just the two of them, him getting fatter and fatter and her wasting down to nothing.

Harvey pulled the car up to the corner of Beechwood and Wallace in front of the modest clapboard house, pale blue with black shutters: the house where he'd grown up and where he lived now, a man in his sixties. Theirs, now, but really his since he'd taken her to Maplewood Acres. Once a week he had visited her, had lunch with her, though she hardly ate and mostly couldn't get out of bed. They watched TV together. He kissed her cheek, said "See you next week." She stared at the flickering TV as if he wasn't there.

"You took away my house," she'd often say.

And now, impossible to believe, she was gone.

He pulled on the brake and sat back for a moment

at the curb, tired after his busy day at the hardware store. So many customers with problems to solve— Mrs. Russell with a backed-up sink drain; Joe Klein needing a special cut of wood; Mary O'Leary unable to rewind her weed whacker. That was the best part of his job, helping people. And between customers, big shipments to get onto the shelves. Dog tired. He leaned back against the headrest and turned his head toward the window. The front yard was covered with red and yellow leaves that needed raking up. He'd have raked them by now if she was still here. This weekend—this weekend he would get them up. Meantime, it was time to get himself out of the car.

Instead, his eyes followed the brick path up to the house, where, framed in the shadows of the open door, he saw his mother standing, arms folded across her chest. His heart pounded hard. He squinted. Her head was small, old, her thin, gray hair pulled tight back, her face wrinkled, dark and almost fleshless like one of those Egyptian mummies he'd seen in a book. She couldn't really be there, but there she stood. She peered at him with a look so hostile he felt breathless.

He pulled the key from the ignition, keeping his eye on his mother. He opened his door and in one movement shoved his seat back and heaved himself, belly first, out of the car. Finally, he looked away and leaned into the back of the car, supporting himself with his hand splayed out on the seat. He rummaged in his toolbox until he found his hammer. This he grasped tightly as he walked toward the house. He kept his eyes on the ground.

"You took away my house."

He could feel her words, her breath in his ear, and now, halfway to her, he looked again toward the front door. It was shut, a shaft of light from the dying sun slicing it in two, and no one was there. No one. He stopped. Maybe she was inside, trying to shut him out. He brought himself up onto the front porch, shifted the hammer from his right hand to his left. He reached for the door latch but let his right arm drop. Instead, he leaned to the left on the railing and peered into the living room window. He could just make out in the dusky light the dark shape of the sofa, the armchair and recliner, the table piled with circulars and catalogues. No one.

He heard himself breathing, felt his heart in his chest. He grabbed the latch, clicked it, opened the door, and stepped inside. In front of him were the steps to the second floor, scuffed dark wood, silent. To his left the door, open, to the living room, to his right the archway between the entry and the dining room.

He pictured her in the kitchen: through the dining room, through the swinging door he loved to push back and forth as a boy. He imagined himself moving into the kitchen and she would be in there, sitting at the kitchen table, terrible.

He told himself he was being cowardly. He forced himself to move through the dining room to the swinging door, which he kicked open. It caught and stayed open, but by now it was dark, too dark to see. He stood outside the kitchen and ran his hand along the doorframe, feeling around on the kitchen wall until he felt the light switch. The sudden glow revealed his mother's big maple table, the two chairs, his coffee mug still there from this morning, the big white enamel sink under the windows, the darkened knotty pine cabinets, the fridge, the stove. She was here. Even though he couldn't see her, he felt her sitting, looking at him. Not in one place. She was everywhere.

The light inside blackened the outside and now he imagined someone out there, someone he couldn't see, looking in. He cocked his head. Surely that was someone—her? Scratching on the screen. He heard nothing but his breathing, his nose whistling, so heavy, so hard, he felt himself suffocating. He stood, with his arms hanging loosely at his sides, hammer in hand. Then he heard the scratching again. He shrank back to the dining room, where she couldn't see him, then heard it again, the familiar sound of the apple tree branch against the kitchen screen. He felt a wave go through his bowels.

He had to get out of the house, couldn't go upstairs, finish looking. Except for the light in the kitchen, some of it spilling into the dining room, the house was dark, black. Now his heart pounded in his temples. He turned and crashed back through the dining room, dropping his hammer in the foyer. He burst through the front door. He lumbered down the path to his car, threw himself in and slammed the door. Started up the motor and drove away.

He drove out of town in one direction, then back to his neighborhood, and out again in another with no destination in mind. He thought of just showing up at Mary's. Mary always said the right thing, Mary liked him and always made him feel good. But what would he say to her?

It took an hour for his heartbeat to get back to normal. He breathed the air coming through the window, rested his arm on the window frame. His mother—had been there. He'd seen her with his own eyes. Seen her in the doorway. He would call Maplewood Acres tomorrow.

Harvey drove all night. He felt safe moving in his car. He stopped at a diner for coffee and a doughnut, and when he returned to the car he looked in the back, on the seats and the floor. He pulled a flashlight out of his toolbox, flashed it around the trunk and across the floor of the front seat before he got in. Even so, as he drove back toward his neighborhood, he couldn't shake the feeling of someone lurking in the back, behind him.

Light was spreading through the spaces between the bare tree branches when he finally pulled up in front of his house. He couldn't now imagine the feeling of terror he'd had, the feeling of the house choking him. As he opened the front door, he was weak with relief. The living room was still in shadow, but the early sun streamed in through the sidelights in the hall, through the front windows in the dining room. The furniture sat squarely on the floor, the frayed edges of the rug undisturbed under the table—the Oriental that his mother had inherited and highly treasured. And the dining table and chairs were special heirlooms, too.

Oak. The big round table could seat six, but there had never been six. His mother's sister sometimes, his cousin who made fun of him. That was all. Maybe way, way back his father? He couldn't know.

He was tired. His eyes felt swollen; he was weak with fatigue. He glanced into the empty kitchen, then turned back to the hall stairs. His hammer lay on the floor. Holding steady against the wall he bent sideways as far as he could, swiping at the handle, catching the hammer up in his hand. He placed it on the hall table. How stupid of him, grabbing this hammer. What had he been thinking? His imagination had got the better of him, was all. Straightening up, he held onto the banister as step by step, a little out of breath, he made his way upstairs.

Her door was always closed, as it was now. From the day he'd taken her to Maplewood Acres, he'd not gone in, just left it as it had been. But now he opened it and stepped in.

Everything was as it had been. In the middle of the room, covered with the worn, flowered print coverlet, stood the iron bedstead. The rag rug that he thought she would have taken with her lay on the floor by the bed. The walls were still a pale green. The doorframe and kickboards, unpainted, revealed a time-darkened pine. He opened the closet door. Dusty and empty. The dresser, empty, felt now like a monstrosity in wood. Almost black with age, its brass drawerpulls guarding drawers shut tight and mysterious, like when he was a child. Back then, he knew the contents of the drawers by heart: hills of silky fabric, underthings— bras and panties—nightgowns, blouses. The shallow top drawer, too high for him without a chair to stand on, was full of small boxes containing safety pins, tiny gold and big silver ones, bobby pins and hairpins, buttons, dimes and nickels and pennies—these he sometimes stole—and in its own box a silver cross with Jesus on it, his head drooping to one side. The dresser was always alluring and he rummaged through it when she was out, prickling with fear that she would return and catch him. He remembered the thrill of opening each drawer and sometimes, because the drawers were stuck, having to yank at the pulls, the harsh scrape of the drawers adding to his fear. But his excitement always ended in disappointment, as if he expected something and didn't find it.

Now he opened them one by one. Nothing. Musty, dry. He bumped his body against them and shoved them back into place, and left the room, closing the door behind him.

He went into the bathroom and pulled back the shower curtain in one big whoosh, revealing the empty tub, stained green around the drain. He opened the medicine chest and grazed his eyes across the few familiar bottles and jars. He opened the linen closet and noted with satisfaction the small piles of worn towels and washcloths. Everything was as it should be. The whole house except the north side was now flooded with sun. Everything was normal.

The door to his own room was open. His walls were green like his mother's but his bed was a special mattress on a platform. He'd had an old iron bedstead, too, the match to his mother's, but once he began to weigh more than 250 pounds, he couldn't sleep on it any more. That was when he got the extra big recliner, too, and the special chair in the kitchen.

He lowered himself onto his bed, his knees hurting, and lay on his back. His neck and shoulders ached and he had to shift around to ease the pain. From driving all night, he thought. And then he fell asleep.

The sound of the telephone ripped through the blackness of his sleep, of his dream, of his memory: the dog at the beach straining against its leash toward him, its teeth flashing, his mother standing ankle deep in the water, and himself falling into the lake, pounding the rubber tube to drown out the kids' laughter, pounding and laughing, no, not laughing but crying, tears squeezing down his fat cheeks.

He lay there for a moment, trying to organize himself. He opened his eyes to bright daylight, maybe past noon. He rolled onto his side and lowered his legs to the floor. Dread spread through his body like a stain. Who could be calling?

Again the telephone rang. He pictured it downstairs where it hung on the kitchen wall. He should get a telephone for the upstairs, he thought as he made his way to it.

"Hello?"

"Hey Harvey, it's Jim."

Harvey looked over at the round kitchen clock on the wall. 12:15. He wasn't due at the store until one today.

"Jim, yeah. Hi. Something up?"

"Not much. You remember Nancy's kid is coming in next week to work for the summer? Looks like he's coming in today. We got the date wrong. So I thought I'd give you a heads-up since you're going to be his, well, you know, you're going to train him."

"Today, huh? How old is he anyway?"

"Must be sixteen. Junior in the fall. Up at the vocational high school."

"Like me!" Harvey said.

"Huh. I guess that's so. "

"Well, I'll see you at one, then. Thanks for the heads-up."

He hung up, but didn't move. If he was going to call Maplewood Acres, he should do it now, he thought, glancing at the clock again. And then he could go to work and forget about it.

He took down the grimy phone book from the shelf over the kitchen cabinet and looked up the number.

"Hello? Angela here. May I help you?"

"This is Harvey Granby," he said, clearing his throat. He thought he sounded like a foghorn and tried to lower his voice. "Is Mrs. O'Connor there?"

"One moment please."

He stretched the phone wire across the kitchen, grabbed his chair, and pulled it over by the phone. He sat down.

"Mr. Granby. This is Mrs. O'Connor. How can I help you?"

"I'm calling about my mother," he said.

"Your mother?"

"Yes," he said, "I'm calling…I'm calling…to see if she's, to check with you." Harvey couldn't think of better words to say what he wanted to know. It hadn't come out right. He waited in a silence that followed.

"Mr. Granby," Mrs. O'Connor finally said. "My dear Mr. Granby, your mother isn't here…she, she passed away…a week ago. She was very sick? Don't you remember, Mr. Granby?"

"Yes, of course I do," Harvey said quickly, embarrassed. "It's just that I have the feeling that she…that she's still there, here." He wanted to hang up now.

"Oh Mr. Granby," she said, "it takes time. It takes time. You miss her is all. It takes time."

"Yes, well, thank you Mrs. O'Connor. I'm sorry I bothered you."

"Not at all. No bother at all," Mrs. O'Connor said.

Harvey hung up the phone and sat back in his chair. He saw himself, clear as day, standing with his aunt and cousin and some folks from the hardware store and the people from Maplewood Acres, standing in the green grass at the graveside while the minister said his words. And he remembered that all he could think of as they lowered the coffin, all he wanted to do, was to open it, to see her in there, to make sure that it was her. That's what he remembered.

He looked up at the clock. He had to go.

The low building with its own parking lot marked by a row of bright red burning bushes along the front was cool and pleasantly dark inside.

"Afternoon, Mary," Harvey said to the ruddy-faced, white-haired woman at the front of the store behind the cash register.

"Hi there, big fella." Mary always called him "big fella" and he liked it. After all, he was big, and the way she said it was like a compliment. Mary had been here even longer than he. Forty years ago, as an afterschool job, he began working at the store. And when he graduated with his automotive diploma, a full-time job awaited him. It was the only job he'd ever had. By now, he was one of three long-timers who pretty much ran the place. He never did open his own car shop like he had planned, but he worked on customers' cars on the side in his yard. Not so much any more, though. He was lucky. Mr. Rosenfeld, who owned the store for all those years before he retired, was good to his employees, made sure of their pensions and health benefits and paid fair wages. With his income and extra money from fixing cars and his mother's Social Security, they hadn't made out badly at all.

"Where's the kid who's starting today?"

"Out in the back. Jim's with him. They're unloading. You had lunch Harvey? I'm just going out." Mary waited, smiling at him.

Harvey stopped. He heard Mary but saw his mother standing at the front door, so clear, handing him his lunch as he went off to work. The feeling of dread rippled through him. These memories, they kept coming on him like this, from nowhere. Then left him, vanished, disappeared, left him, teasing.

"Hamburger'n coke would be fine, thanks Mary."

He moved on to the back room of the store.

"Hey Harvey," Jim called out. Harvey waved.

Through the big outdoor opening at the far end of the room, pushing a dolly piled high with bags of soil, a young boy shuffled in—soft, pudgy-looking with buzzed hair and fat pants—like me when I was a kid, Harvey thought.

"This here is Mr. Granby," Jim said. "He's the one you'll be reporting to. He turned to Harvey. "Billy's his name."

The boy stopped and smiled tentatively.

"I see Jim's put you to work. Go ahead with those bags, then. When you're done we'll take a tour of the store. You gotta familiarize yourself with everything we sell in the different departments so that's where we'll start. You'll be here three afternoons a week, right?"

"Yes. Three to five on Mondays and Thursdays. One to four on Wednesdays," the boy croaked. *Voice was still changing,* Harvey thought. As he turned away, he heard Mr. Rosenfeld telling him, clear as on that first day: "You have to get to know every product on every shelf so you can help customers," he'd said as they walked up and down the aisles.

For the next hour, Jim had Billy moving bags of soil and compost from the supply room to the walkway outside. The boy worked hard, sweated in the cool day as if it were midsummer, and arrived back up front to report to Harvey, his face streaked with dirt. Won't be so pudgy working here, Harvey thought.

He began the tour of the store with the gardening section.

"You have a garden at home?"

"My Mom does."

"You seem to know a lot. You help out?"

"Yeah. For my allowance."

"What do you do?"

"Mow. Weed whack. Mulch. Dig up stuff so my mom can replant it somewhere else. Stuff like that."

"You like doing it?"

"It's okay."

"You know next to nothing about cars, I bet."

"I'm starting automotive next semester. And I'm learning how to drive."

"If you're gonna get your license, you better learn something about cars, about the insides, how they work. You ride a bike?"

"Yeah."

"You know how to fix it? You know, if the chain comes off or the wheel freezes or you get a flat?"

"Mostly."

"Who taught you?"

"My mom."

"Not your dad?"

"Naw. My dad lives in Pennsylvania. He's got a new family." Billy looked down at the floor.

"So your mom knows how to fix a bike?"

"My mom knows a lotta things."

After Billy left, Harvey went back to the front, where

a line had formed at the cash register.

"Hey, Harvey, how's it goin'?" a customer at the end of the line said, putting his hand on Harvey's arm. "Sorry about your mother," he lowered his voice. "I just heard. It's a big loss, a mother, a big loss."

"Yes," Harvey said. "Thanks, Frank. Appreciate it." Then he called out to Mary, "I'm going to be in the back straightening out a mess in Aisle 5. Jim's outside. Call me if you need me."

As he organized the hoses on one shelf and began stacking boxes of fertilizer on another, he looked up to see a woman coming slowly toward him from the far end of the aisle. She was old and moved with difficulty. He braced himself against the shelf to straighten up. Her face was dark and wrinkled like his mother's, a thought he tried to sweep away. But the visage of his mother persisted and he remembered how she sometimes came to the store to buy something instead of asking him to bring it home. Not often, but she liked to come to the store and gossip with Mary. Mary was more his age than his mother's—only ten years older—but the two women had something in common. They complained about men, how they left you high and dry. Mary's husband left when she was still young, before she had any children. She never remarried. So they made jokes about how men were. Mary would say how lucky his mother was to have a good, reliable son like Harvey. Harvey felt proud when Mary said those things, always hoped his mother would notice. But he also felt something else, not proud, that he couldn't name, as the two of them went on talking and laughing harshly about the unreliability of men.

"You know, Harvey, you should find yourself a girl and get married," Mary would sometimes say. Harvey felt his face flush, felt embarrassed when Mary went on at him like that in front of his mother.

"No girl would look at me," he'd finally mutter, hoping she would stop.

"Take a look around you boy," she'd say. "Are all the married people you see like models out of some magazine, huh? Like celebrities on the TV? No siree. Some of 'em are downright ugly. You're a big, strong, gentle man, Harvey; there's plenty of girls would be glad and lucky to have you."

She'd always end by singing and dancing around a little:

For every boy there is a girl,
For every dream there is a real world.
For every lip there is a kiss,
For every cheek there is a caress.

And his mother, smiling a little, would say, "Oh Mary, stop that silly song."

All that was a long time ago, but it always made him like Mary, maybe better than anyone else.

Harvey helped the woman with the dark face, who wasn't so old after all. He finished stacking and pricing the boxes of fertilizer and then went to the office. This was a nine o'clock night. He would spend the rest of his shift going through invoices. Jim and Gus, who was due in any minute, would take care of customers. He was dog tired and hoped they wouldn't need him. It felt good to ease himself down into his padded chair and just go through papers.

It wasn't that he didn't think about girls. He did. In high school there were Sally and Jane and Frances, especially, and he thought about them and they filled his head when he lay in bed and pleasured himself. He was very bold in his imagination. But in real life he passed them in the halls, sat next to them in class and never looked at them. Only in his secret life could he really see them, feel them. And later there were women, certain customers, a pretty neighbor with two children and a husband who lived across the street; he worked on their Saab. And there was Mary. What a surprise it was when Mary pushed her way into his imaginings in his bedroom, surrounded him, touched him, smiled in his face. Even now he sometimes pleasured himself with Mary.

Sometimes, he remembered, he would suddenly hear some noise outside his room and he would lie there, still, sure that his mother was about to burst into his room, about to catch him at what he was doing. He never felt alone, even at night with his door shut. He was aware of her even when she wasn't in the house, was downtown shopping or out cleaning someone's house, or visiting with her sister. Then, when the house was empty, he never stopped wondering when she would be back. He didn't miss her exactly, but he felt an absence. She took care of him. Made his meals, his bed, laundered his clothes. They watched TV together, went to the movies with Mary or sometimes Jim and his wife. But he never knew when she would suddenly turn on him, ridicule him, like that day on the beach when she called him a dummy and didn't care that he was scared.

He leaned back in his chair. She was gone now. She had died. He remembered. The coffin closed up tight. He couldn't see her.

He picked up a sheaf of papers and tapped their

bottoms on the desk until they were all straightened out. He placed them in a folder, then placed the folder in the file drawer. He yawned and looked at his watch. It was 8:45, almost time to go home. He looked forward to the day after tomorrow when Billy would be back and he would be sort of like a father to him.

Harvey pulled up to his house right in front of the path to the front door, then sat for a minute in the car before pushing open the door, shoving his seat back, and swinging his legs out onto the road. Pulling himself up out of the car seat, he rounded the nose of his car and started up the walk, noting that the streetlight was out. It was very dark, no moon, hard to see. He began to feel uneasy, first, with the sensation that there was someone behind him, then something more general, a dread like the dread he had felt last night and this afternoon when the phone rang. *Oh God, please don't let me be afraid,* he said to himself just the way he used to say those words when he was a boy, when he had done something bad and would pray not to get caught, but mostly at night when he was in his bedroom and it was so dark and he heard noises and felt presences, imagined snakes under his bed.

"Oh God, please don't let me be afraid," he prayed every night after his mother told him that he couldn't come into her room and sleep with her any more.

"You're too old. You're too old to be afraid of the dark."

So he had spent night after night in a sweat of terror before finally falling, exhausted, asleep. The terror became a part of the process of going to sleep. Somewhere along the line, it had stopped, he'd outgrown it.

How could he feel this way now, all these years later?

He tried to remember where he had put his hammer, but immediately felt ridiculous, cowardly. He went forward anyway, clicked the latch with his thumb and pushed the door open, reaching out to the wall on his right to flip the switch. The light filled the entryway, shone halfway up the stairs and into the dining room and living room.

He went into the living room and sat down in his recliner, his whole body—skin, eyes, ears—in a heightened state of alertness.

He picked up the remote. He'd drown out this sense of an unseen presence with the TV. He switched it on, watched an ad for a Chevy Blazer. "A crummy car," he thought. Soon, however, the television noise receded into the background as he slipped into the memory of how he used to come home every night and have his supper, alone, at the kitchen table, while his mother, who ate earlier, moved around the kitchen doing things that made no sense to him, wiping off a clean counter, taking out forks or spoons from a drawer and putting them back in some rearrangement, taking down the dish towel from the towel rack, refolding it and laying it back over the rack. And when he was done eating, she'd wash up his dishes while he took out the trash or straightened out the papers and magazines destined for the recycling container. Then they'd watch television, he in his recliner and she on the sofa, often knitting or crocheting, not even looking at the screen.

Suddenly, his face was wet with tears. He bent forward, his shoulders shaking, and sobbed into his open hands until his tears stopped flowing and he could breathe again, until his body sank back into itself.

"I gotta stop this," he thought. He wanted it to stop, all of it. His mind to stop. To get up and do something, not sit around and mope. He should do something, and stop thinking.

He thought about Gus, his best friend at Weston Voc. Gus's mother was kind of sickly, pale and silent, and his father was a drunk. He owned the cigar store and everyone knew he was drunk half the time. Harvey knew that his red bumpy face was somehow connected with the paper cup he kept next to the cash register. Gus was always getting out of his father's way, wandering around town. Everyone watched out for him. Gus ate at Harvey's a lot and Harvey's mother stuffed him with food, too. Harvey knew he, Harvey, was lucky. And Gus was unlucky, but he never acted unlucky. Gus had lots of friends and wherever he was there were other kids and lots of talking and laughing and punching in a friendly way. Harvey joined in but he always felt, deep inside him, that something was wrong with him that they would notice. Whenever he had this thought, that something was wrong with himself, he thought of his mother, as if what was wrong with him was her. But his mother was normal, not like Gus's mother. She did all the things that mothers did. She was never irresponsible like Gus's mother. Harvey's mother loved him and took good care of him. Except sometimes when other people were around, those times she turned on him. When she called him a dummy like that day at the beach, or laughed when Mary said lots of girls would be glad to have him. He remembered those most; they stayed inside him.

"You took away my house," she'd said. But he hadn't. He hadn't taken away her house. She was sick, dying, and they, together, put the house in his name. It was her idea. And he took her to Maplewood Acres because he couldn't take care of her any more.

Harvey pulled himself out of his recliner. He turned on the hall light in the entryway, went up the stairs and into his mother's room. Once there, he began to pull the half-open drawers out of the dresser, easing them, as they stuck, from side to side. He piled them carefully, one on top of the other, on the bare floor. Then he hoisted the dresser on his back, straining forward—it was solid oak. He made his way slowly down the stairs, grunting, resting the legs on the stair above him with each step. He stood the dresser in the hallway. It took two more trips to get the drawers down. He upended them against the wall. Tomorrow he would put the dresser together on the front lawn. He would add the Oriental rug and the maple kitchen set. He would go to the basement and paint a sign, "Free Stuff," on an old piece of wood. He would prop it up against the dresser. For now, he would go upstairs to bed and get himself some good sleep.

The next day was one of his Saturdays off, so he had time to finish his plan. He put the items out on the lawn, the sign "Free Stuff" propped up against the dresser. He bet everything would be gone by noon. The kitchen felt roomy without the table and chairs; they always took up too much space, made it hard to get to the sink, the fridge. He would get a small round table.

He finished his second cup of coffee and a big hunk of the walnut coffee cake he'd gotten at the supermarket, the same cake that his mother always bought on Friday night for a weekend treat. He got up, rinsed out his cup, put it in the dish drain, closed the unfinished cake in its box and wiped the crumbs off the table with a sponge. He was fussing in the kitchen, he thought, just like his mother. Then he sat down on his chair and contemplated the telephone, hesitating before he dialed the number.

"Hi Mary," he said when she answered.

"Well hi there, big fella. What can I do for you on your day off?"

"I was wondering, Mary, if you would like to go to the movies tonight. The science fiction one at the mall. Have pizza first and go to the movies."

"Well. I'd like that, Harvey, I sure would."

He sat for a while. Then he got up and went outside to the shed in the side yard. Choosing from among the tools leaning against the dark interior wall, he grabbed his bamboo rake. He glanced out toward the front yard: the furniture was gone and the sign lay face down on the walkway to the front door. He walked across the lawn and began raking, tumbling the red and yellow leaves into long lines across the lawn.

Most Original

"So, girls, have you decided what you want to be this year?" Mr. Turner was a really tall man who always bent forward a little, as if he was trying to get closer to all the shorter people around him. He looked first at Susie, then at me.

I turned to Susie, but she just shrugged: "I haven't decided yet."

"And how about you, Annie, do you have an idea?"

"I was thinking about being an Eskimo," I said without thinking. We had just finished up the Eskimos in school. I didn't want to sound like someone with no ideas. But I had no idea how I would "be" an Eskimo.

"Hmmm," was all Mr. Turner said.

"That's a neat idea," Susie said. "How about you be an Eskimo and I'll be a polar bear?"

Susie's father was an architect. We were in his studio on the top floor of their house. I'd been to Susie's lots of times, but never in Mr. Turner's studio. It was the biggest room in anybody's house I'd ever seen, full of rows and piles of supplies for his drawings and little models of houses on shelves. There were fat cardboard tubes that looked like umbrella stands on the bare, wooden floor, stacks of white graph paper on wall shelves. I especially liked his drafting table, the way it tilted forward. On it was a big piece of white paper with sketches of a house that had a flat roof and big windows. He even drew little trees with green smudges for the leaves. I was dying to sit on his high stool and draw pictures.

Everything looked so neat and interesting, not at all like my father's study at home. My father didn't have anything in his study, really, except books in bookshelves and piled on the floor. And his Underwood typewriter on a typewriter table with stacks of typing paper on one side. And his yellow pads, legal pads he called them, covered with his scribbly handwriting you couldn't read. He was a writer. He often wrote in his pajamas.

"Well," Mr. Turner said after a while, "those are both great ideas girls, really great, but wouldn't it be even more distinctive, more unusual—if you want to win the prize, you know, you want to have an idea no one has thought of—if, let's see, you, Susie, were a totem pole instead of a polar bear and Annie was—"

"I don't want to be a totem pole," Susie said quickly. "I want to be a polar bear. No one is going to think of it and I am going to be a polar bear."

And that was how I came to be a totem pole on the night before Halloween, 1945.

I thought this Halloween would be like every other Halloween, something my older sister and I did together. But when she all of a sudden announced that she was too old for Halloween and was having a sleepover at Ginny's house instead, I was so disappointed. It felt like she was getting too old for everything, and leaving me behind. Without her, Halloween wouldn't be any fun at all. There was a lot about Halloween that wasn't all that much fun anyway. It came every year and everyone talked about it—"What're you gonna be for Halloween?" I never knew very far ahead like the other kids.

And so, every year I got all sweaty beneath my mask. The slit for my mouth got wet and mushy from my hot breath. The mask was made of some junky material and smelled horrible. Our costumes were whatever they had at Murphy's Department Store, like a ghost or a witch. We always got them at the last minute. And then we went to Town Hall and kids marched around in a circle for the contest for Most Original and Scariest Costume. I knew I'd never get a prize, and, anyway, I didn't care about winning. My parents thought there shouldn't be a Halloween contest. They didn't believe in contests for children.

But there was one really great thing about

Halloween, and that was doing it with my sister. We had so much fun just trying on one mask or costume after another. Sometimes we almost peed in our pants we laughed so hard. She always did great makeup and one year she won the prize for Most Original when she went as a mermaid that she made herself. Our aunt, who was visiting, helped her. But now she wasn't going with me and I would have to do it alone.

So I was glad when Susie invited me to stay with her and make our costumes. I had never made my own costume and I didn't know how, but she said her parents would help us. Susie's costumes were always fabulous, different from anybody's. She'd won Most Original last year and the year before. Sometimes I felt a little jealous, but I didn't really think about winning myself. I just thought her costumes were neat.

We followed Mr. Turner into his studio and he began pulling huge sheets of stiff cardboard off his shelves.

"Okey-doke," he said. "Let's get started." He measured me from my shoulders to my knees. Humming, he spread the sheet out on his big table and cut it with a box cutter, then bent it around me from my shoulders to my knees. It was very stiff and kept springing open.

"Susie," he called across the room. "Come hold this while I draw a line." When he was finished he laid the cardboard out on his table and pulled up one edge to line up with the line he'd drawn, making a cylinder. I wondered what he was doing, but he just kept humming. He told Susie and me to hold the cylinder together while he taped it with long strips of black tape on both sides, top to bottom three times. Then he stapled the top and bottom. He stood it on the floor. I didn't quite get what he was doing and I wondered what was next.

Mrs. Turner joined us too. She was a small woman with gray hair and a wrinkled, pink face who looked much older than my mother.

"I think I have just the thing for your polar bear, Susie," she said, "something I've been wondering what to do with." She was carrying a big pile of white, furry fabric from her sewing room. She draped it over different parts of Susie until only her round, chubby face showed. Susie grinned and growled.

"This is going to be fun."

Her mother pinned the fur in several places.

"I think we'll do her head with papier mâché." Mr. Turner stepped back and nodded. I couldn't believe my ears! I thought that papier mâché was something you could only do in school.

"We have a small beach ball in the garage that's just the ticket," she said. "And once it dries we can puncture the ball and build the nose and ears out from the head. It'll dry tonight and we can paint it tomorrow."

"I want to do the papier mâché," Susie said.

"Well, right now you can tear up that pile of newspapers over there in the corner," her mother said as she left the room.

I was hoping that Mr. Turner would give me a job to do, but instead he took me by the shoulders. "Okey-doke," he said. "Let's see how this works, Annie. Keep your arms at your sides, now." And he slipped the cardboard cylinder over my head and down to my knees, smooshing my arms against my body. Then, still humming, he measured me from my shoulder to the top of my head, then pulled out a cardboard tube that he cut to his measurements with a little saw. He placed it over my head, and it fit just inside the cylinder. It was amazing how he made it all work.

My parents never did stuff like this—make things. They played cards with us, and word games and checkers and chess, Monopoly and Clue, but nothing like this. This was going to be fun.

"How does that feel?" he asked, stepping back.

"It's a little tight up by my shoulders," I said. I couldn't see.

"That's good. That'll help keep it from slipping." He lifted the short tube up off my head and back on again, drawing two squares on it, still humming. Then he took it off, cut out the squares, and put it back on my head. The cutouts lined up with my eyes and now I could see, which felt a lot better.

"We'll cover the eyes with red cellophane." He stepped away. "Try to walk," he said.

I shuffled across the room. It felt a little clumsy, but I could do it.

"Perfect." He marked the cardboard and took it away. "I think this is going to work perfectly." I didn't say anything because I knew he wasn't talking to me.

"I'm bored," Susie tore newspaper strips, let them fall to the floor.

"Just give me a few minutes," her father said. "I want to get this right." He fussed with the cardboard, yanked me this way and that, and asked me if it was too tight.

"After dinner you can both work on painting the totem pole. I'll work with you on the details." He paused and looked at the tubes. "This is going to be a great costume. You'll be sorry, Susie, that you didn't want to be the totem pole."

"I like being a polar bear better."

"Well, tomorrow," her father said, "when the papier mâché has dried you can paint the face. I'll work on the mouth and nose. We'll get a perfect bear face."

Susie's parents worked on our costumes until dinnertime. They had discussions with each other about which way would be best to put together some parts of the bear costume and what to paint on the totem pole.

After dinner Mrs. Turner found a book in their library about North American art. She and Mr. Turner compared different pictures of totem poles and held them up for us to see. It seemed so funny to me how they were talking so much and looking at pictures for our Halloween costumes.

"What do you think of this one?" Mr. Turner asked, pointing to a picture of a red, black, and green totem pole that represented an ancestor. The face looked ferocious, with a wide, fat mouth outlined thickly in red and green. Susie's parents liked this totem pole the best. Susie and I said we liked it, too.

"You know," Mr. Turner said, "I think we're going to end up with two pretty original costumes. Which one do you think might win?"

The next day, Halloween, when all the work was done, Mr. and Mrs. Turner helped us get into our costumes. Susie's body was soon covered with the shaggy, white material her mother had sewn into a kind of bag with legs and arms and her father fitted the huge bear head onto Susie's head. She disappeared completely under it, looking ferocious with a big, toothy mouth. She walked around the living room stabbing the air with her "paws" and laughing and growling into the hollow head, looking through the two black holes for her eyes. She looked great.

I stood straight while Susie's father and mother fitted the cardboard tube over my head and pulled it down to my shoulders; I had to keep my elbows a little bent out to make sure it wouldn't slip. They placed the head over my head, turning it around until I could see through the long eye slits, now covered with red cellophane.

They stood back and surveyed what I could not see: a four-foot-five totem pole with a fierce-looking face, an ancestor, painted shiny black by Susie and me, over which Mr. Turner had painted two arms and hands with spread fingers in red and green straight down each side. On the head he had made a huge mouth outlined in red, then green. I hoped that Susie and I would get to do more of the painting, but Mr. Turner wanted to get it just right so we just did the background. They took me over to a mirror so I could see. It looked great. I had to turn my whole self around, shuffling with my feet, to see Susie, who was still sort of dancing around and laughing. I started to laugh, too. She gave a big roar in my direction.

This was going to be fun.

"You look the best," she said. "I betcha you're going to get Most Original."

I smiled, but remembered that she couldn't see me. I was invisible, locked in the dark and no one, except the Turners, had any idea who I was.

"If this doesn't win a prize," I heard Mr. Turner say to Susie's mother, "you'll have to wonder about the judges."

And suddenly I felt a scared thrilled feeling in my body. I was dying, aching to win the prize.

Susie's parents hadn't thought about the fact that I couldn't sit in the car because I couldn't bend, but they didn't want me to put the costume on at the Town Hall. The whole point of Halloween was to be unrecognizable. So they put Susie in the front with them and, as Mr. Turner said, "Okey-doke, heave ho!" they lifted me into the back seat and laid me out like a plank.

When we reached Town Hall they hauled me out again and Mr. Turner made some adjustments, then walked with me to the door.

The big main room, where the town meetings took place, was crowded with kids in costumes, some store-bought, some just pulled together, like mine always were, and some of them amazing, like ours. I could see lots of ghosts in white sheets with big round holes for eyes. There were some kids with nothing on but rubber masks—of Frankenstein or the Green Hornet, Wonder Woman or Roy Rogers—from Murphy's; lots of witches, too, with yellow brooms and pointy black hats; ballet dancers in sparkling white tutus and made-up faces. I saw a beautiful Snow White with a fluffy black wig and lots of makeup; I was pretty sure that it was Sandra, but with all the makeup I couldn't really tell. And I saw a sickly green Dracula with huge fangs who I thought might be Victor Wolk, because he had Victor's funny walk. A few parents had costumes on, too, and marched in the parade, something my parents always said was foolish. Some parents were over by the big bucket where kids were bobbing for apples. Mostly parents were standing around talking with each other and calling out to their kids to behave themselves, stop running around. As usual, it was pretty noisy and disorganized.

I missed my sister. I wished she was with me, wished she could see me in my costume. I would put it on for her at home, later, after my parents picked me up.

There were long tables in the back of the room with piles of doughnuts and lots of apple cider. I really wanted a doughnut, but there was no way for me to have one without taking my head off. People kept coming up to me and saying "Wow, that's a really great costume," and asking who I was. Once I said in a big low voice, "I am the Totem Pole," but then I stopped. I didn't want anyone to guess. Susie cavorted around me, growling and pawing the air. It was a lot of fun, the best Halloween party.

Finally the littlest kids were herded into a big circle and the mothers in charge played a record of Halloween songs. Some of the kids looked scared and didn't smile or laugh. Some even cried like babies and looked around in panic for their mothers. That happened every year. And some wandered out of the circle and their mothers pushed them gently back in. Everyone clapped. They were too young for a contest so they each got a prize of a little bag of candy. I thought it was nice that they all got a prize. My parents didn't believe in prizes unless everyone got one.

When it was time for the older kids, the room was cleared and we made a big circle in the center. Susie and I stood next to each other, and her mother, with a big grin, hugged Susie and knocked on my costume.

"Break a leg," she said in a big, loud voice. I thought she must have meant to say, "Don't break a leg," because it was so hard for me to shuffle around the room.

As we started to move with the music, I felt so excited. I shuffled to keep up with Susie, enjoying the sensation of being not myself, but a totem pole.

We moved around in a circle before the judges, who sat at a long table at the front of the room: Mr. Davenport, the boys' librarian, who we all thought was a woman in disguise; Mr. Wilding, the minister at St. Matthew's Parish; Miss Fisk, the principal of the Center School, my school; Mr. Murphy and Mr.

Peretti, Town Selectmen; and Mr. Davis, who was the athletic coach at the high school. They all came down and watched us go by one by one. We went around again. They watched us and talked to each other. They wrote words down on little cards.

I could only think about winning.

Finally, the music stopped and we all stood still. The judges got together at their table and passed their cards back and forth.

Mr. Wilding stood up. Everyone was quiet.

"This has been a very hard year for us judges," he said in a loud voice. "There are so many wonderful, clever, scary costumes. We wish we could give a prize to all of you, but then," he laughed, "that wouldn't be a contest, would it?" Mr. Wilding said the same thing every year.

"So we've come to an agreement about the two first prizes. For the scariest costume, this year's prize goes…" He walked over to the green Dracula and touched him on the shoulder. Dracula took off his face mask and it was Victor, just like I thought. Everyone cheered and clapped. Victor smiled and blushed. Mr. Wilding handed him an envelope with the prize, a $25 war bond, in it. Everyone clapped again.

"Congratulations," Mr. Wilding said, and

Victor's mother came over and hugged him.

When everyone quieted down, Mr. Wilding shouted "… and for the most original costume…" he walked toward the circle, right over to me and touched, then tapped my costume. I couldn't take off my head like Victor did on account of my arms being pinned to my sides, but the head was lifted off me and there was Mr. Turner smiling and nodding as Mr. Wilding called my name and, since my hands were in the totem pole, he handed Mr. Turner my envelope with the $25 bond in it. Everyone was clapping and calling my name.

I had won.

"Congratulations," Mr. Wilding said to me. "And congratulations to all of you for coming here tonight to celebrate All Hallows' Eve with your friends and families. This brings the community together and is the best and safest way to spend Halloween." Mr. Wilding said that every year, too.

The party was over. By then my parents had come to pick me up and I saw them at the door looking for me. I asked Mr. Turner to put the totem pole head back on so they could see it.

Susie was still in her shaggy bear body. She held the ferocious head under her arm. I looked very hard at her. I had worried that she might be annoyed if I won. But she didn't look annoyed at all.

'Thank you, Susie," I said. "The costumes were fun and I had a really neat time at your house."

"You did?" she asked, grinning at me. "My parents get so bossy. I hate being bossed, my dad especially. But at least I didn't win this time. A lot of kids were mad at me last year and said it wasn't fair."

Mostly I was glad she wasn't mad at me, but I thought that maybe they were right, it was unfair that Susie won twice in a row.

My mother arrived and hugged both of us. "How fabulous, both of you, are. Your costume is amazing, Annie, just amazing!" She really meant it.

Mr. Turner took off the head again and slipped the rest of the totem pole up and off.

"I can see that you and Mrs. Turner gave them a lot of guidance," my mother said, "something my husband and I are no good at. All thumbs, both of us," she laughed. "She'll have to go to your house every year, now that her standards are so high."

She turned to me. "But you'll have to tell me, honey, how you did all this."

"Well, Mr. Turner—" I started out.

Mr. Turner turned to me. "We had a fine time working on this, didn't we?" he said, handing me the envelope with my bond. He turned to my mother.

"The idea of Eskimos was all Annie's and that inspired the rest of it, a totem pole and a polar bear. The girls were great and did a fine job. Of course, I had to figure out some of the construction problems, but they were with me all the way and we had a really fine time, didn't we girls?"

I nodded, and we all said our goodbyes. My dad offered to get my suitcase from the Turners' car and followed them to it.

My mom and I watched as Mr. Turner, bending a little toward his wife to catch what she was saying, walked off with a section of the totem pole under each arm.

My sister would never see me in it, I realized with a sudden pang of disappointment—but now I think: perhaps that was for the best.

Gnome

Six children work at the art table, at the far end of the classroom. It's the morning study period and their classmates are also in groups, one working on the daily math, the other on reading. Their teacher circulates around the room, giving help where needed.

Two of the children at the art table work together on a poster of the Dutch buying Manhattan from Native Americans on the shore of the Hudson River.

"Was the Hudson polluted then, too?" David, a solidly built blond boy asks, "or can we paint it blue?" He has been drawing a Dutch ship in the background.

"Nah," says Laura, a thin girl with wispy hair. "It wasn't polluted then because they didn't have any factories."

It's the end of the first month of school. While two of his classmates work on small drawings related to the study of Dutch New York, Ivan, a new student, sits at the other end of the table decorating his writing book. The teacher sits down beside him.

"Did you have art stuff like this in your class at your old school?" David asks.

Ivan looks up. He is small, with big ears and fine brown hair that falls across his forehead. He sits with shoulders hunched and eyes blinking behind glasses, his pale face in concentration on his project. He wears a white dress shirt with a collar and dark pants with a belt. The other children wear jeans and t-shirts.

"Nah." His raspy voice sounds loud for someone so small and pale. Some kids in other parts of the room look up for a moment before returning to their work.

"No. We only did art in the art room. And we all drew the same pictures." Ivan talks very slowly, taking care with each word. "And we wore shirts and ties and jackets."

"Yuck." Then, without looking up from his ship, David asks, "So which school do you like better?"

Ivan glues a piece of pale blue card stock on the cover of his writing book and finishes writing "Ivan's Book of Writing" on the cover. He is poised to make a design with a red marker, but pauses, thinking.

"Well," he drawls, "some things are better about my old school and some are better here."

"So, which things?" David paints blue water, while Laura, who looks up, works with a skinny brush on the Native American figure on the shore.

"I like the kids better here," Ivan says. "Much better. You know what they used to call me at my old school?" The children across from him, silently working, look up, suddenly alert.

The teacher puts her arm on Ivan's shoulder.

"You might not want to say what they called you," she whispers.

Ivan looks up at her. His eyes blink once behind his glasses and then he turns back to his gluing.

"What did they call you?" David, leaning forward, asks.

"Oh nothing," Ivan says. "Just Ivan, like here."

"Time to put everything away and get ready for gym," the teacher calls out, and the room fills with the noise of scraping chairs and feet on the floor.

The Orange Coat

Shopping with her stepmother was not what Delia wanted to be doing. But when Elly offered to take her to Ohrbach's coat sale, held every year on the day after Thanksgiving, Delia couldn't think how to say no. Not only was her old winter coat falling apart, it was too small, having been bought almost two years ago when she was twelve. It had been a mistake, mentioning it to Elly.

"I'll take you to Ohrbach's the day after Thanksgiving," she'd said. "It's a real New York experience and we'll find you a perfect coat on sale to boot."

Elly was trying to be nice, maybe, but Delia didn't want to shop with her. She didn't like Elly. Or maybe that wasn't it. Maybe it was more just the fact that Elly had dropped into Delia's life out of nowhere two years ago and now they were supposed to be a family, feel close when they weren't. She was an English teacher at a private high school and always offering to read drafts of Delia's papers, which so far Delia had avoided, but somehow she'd been unable to avoid this.

They hurried along Thirty-Fourth Street in the chill air—Elly, a tall, heavy woman in her early thirties with pale, frizzy hair and big glasses, and Delia, petite and wiry, her dark chestnut hair pulled back, twisted, and clipped to the back of her head.

The entrance to Ohrbach's Department Store was a wide, doorless opening. Overhead vents blew down hot air that kept out cold blasts from West Forty-Second Street. Shoppers passed through this hot wind, then scattered in all directions. Everyone hurried. A clattering wooden escalator carried them to the upper floors and most, along with Elly and Delia, got off at the dimly lit second floor, the coat floor. Here there were already many women trying on coats and tossing the rejects back over the racks, and even onto the floor. It was a madhouse.

In the junior department, young girls paraded in coats for their mothers, who stood back with appraising looks. Delia eyed these girls and their mothers, their ease and closeness, with envy. Usually she shopped with her mother and sister, but Cassy was away at college and her mother, who had moved them from the country to New York in August, was studying for her college degree and had no time. Her mother would have taken her to Best's, the big, white building on Fifth Avenue with green awnings and glass doors, pink and cream dressing rooms with three-way mirrors, and salesladies who told you what suited you. Delia wasn't at all sure that Ohrbach's was the right place to shop.

She turned to Elly, who unbuttoned her coat and ran her fingers through her hair, pulling it out from her head. "What size are you?" Elly asked.

"Usually a six," Delia said, thinking this might embarrass Elly, who was fat and probably wore a sixteen.

"Do you know what you're looking for?"

Delia shrugged. "Not really."

"Surely you have something in mind—a style, color, maybe things to rule out."

"Well, I know I don't want black," Delia said, just to say something. "Probably something classic."

"Tell you what," Elly finally said. "Why don't you go through those "petites" over there while I go through these. I think I have a pretty good idea of what would look good on you and, you know, what's in style."

Delia eyed Elly's bright green coat with huge, glossy black buttons, wide sleeves and fat cuffs. She was pretty sure it was ugly.

"Afterwards, we can go to lunch and you can tell me how your paper on Whitman is coming. I thought we'd go to Hamburger Heaven. You'd like that, wouldn't you?"

"Hamburger Heaven sounds perfect," Delia said, relieved to be on safer ground.

She turned to a long rack of coats and felt overwhelmed. She tried on a dark brown wool with epaulettes and hastily took it off, feeling ridiculous, like an army officer. Another, a classic camel hair, was, she felt sure, not a good color for her. Cassy always said she shouldn't wear anything beigy, and though she couldn't for the life of her see what Cassy saw that was wrong, she had taken this prohibition as her own. With a little regret (she felt reassured by the fact that it was such a classic), she hung it back up. She continued poking through the rack, pulling out a coat here and there, trying it on and hastily hanging it back up, almost without looking, feeling wrong in every coat she tried.

"You're trying on mostly the browns and grays," Elly said. "Why don't you try a color, a navy or maroon, or something brighter. You have the coloring for brighter colors, you know? And you could choose any color, since your clothes tend to be neutral."

Delia looked up but didn't answer.

"Solid, of course. Not plaid, like this one," Elly added. "What I mean is, don't rule something out because of the color. Be a little adventurous; pretend to be someone else and try different colors. Makes it more fun."

She paused, then went on. "Have you seen anything that you might want to consider?"

"Not so far," Delia called out.

"Oh, wait, how about this one. Take a look," Elly held up an orange woolen coat. "It's bold perhaps, but you know, Delia, you could really use more color."

"You said that already," Delia thought, but she smiled and took the coat. She tried it on. It was soft, almost hairy on the outside, like mohair, and was lined with a dark brown pile. She looked doubtfully in the mirror.

"That looks really great on you," Elly said, smiling. "It's amazing how the orange brings out your features, especially your brown eyes. You're very pretty, you know. You don't have to hide it."

Delia turned back to the mirror. The coat was A-shaped, a deep orange with slash pockets and gold buttons. The style was a lot like most of her friends' coats, but the orange was unusual. Maybe her grays and browns were a little mousy, a little boring.

"I don't know…"

She looked at herself from front to side in the mirror. She liked the orange, but thought maybe it wasn't right for a coat. She didn't think Cassy would ever choose it. Maybe it stood out too much. Or maybe it was really handsome and distinctive. She just didn't know. She felt sick with not knowing. She tried to read Elly's response.

"You look terrific, Delia. It's very becoming on you. I just love it."

Delia looked at herself again. She did look good, radiant even. Behind her, reflected in the mirror, were two girls and their mothers standing nearby with coats over their arms, waiting for their turn. Delia wondered what they thought of the orange coat. She studied her image.

"Well," she said, "Yes. I think I like it."

She smiled at Elly, adding, "Yes, I'll take it."

"I'm so pleased," Elly said, then stopped for a moment. "Now you really like it, don't you?"

"I really do," Delia said.

They moved through the shoppers to the long line at the cashier's. Delia paid for the coat with money her mother had given her. The saleslady laid the coat in sheets of tissue paper in a great box, folding them as if she were pulling a blanket up over a baby. She put the top on the box, tied it up, and, adding a handle, presented it to Delia.

As they moved through the store and out onto Seventh Avenue, Elly put her arm around Delia.

"I knew we'd find you something wonderful," she said.

Delia was relieved to have pleased Elly. Or relieved that the hunt was over. She gave Elly a smile as they walked east toward Fifth Avenue and the promised lunch at Hamburger Heaven.

When Delia pulled the coat out of the box and held it up, her mother, hunched as usual over her desk, glanced up.

"Well, that's certainly a new look. It's very nice dear."

"Do you really think so?"

"Put it on… Yes. It is. Handsome. The orange is…a bit of a surprise, but it looks good on you. Did Elly help you choose it?"

"Well, sort of. Not like you and Cassy, but she liked it the best. Do you really like it?"

"Yes, dear. I really do. But the important question is, do you?"

Delia, unconvinced, regarded her mother, who went back to her reading. She wasn't really paying attention. And now that she thought about it, what did Elly's opinion matter? Elly's green coat was ugly— no doubt about that—and she wore those wraparound denim skirts and Ship 'n Shore blouses that Cassy said were unsophisticated. Delia lingered a moment, waiting for her mother to say more, then gave up and went into her bedroom. She tried the coat on again, looking in the full-length mirror on the back of her closet door. She was reassured; it was a perfect fit, very becoming, and she felt attractive in it. Seconds later, though, she thought the coat swallowed her up, that the orange was actually loud. She tore it off and hung it in her closet, pushing the door shut. She hadn't gotten it right.

She sat down on her bed, remembering her first day in her new high school just two months before, in September. The minute she'd walked into the classroom, she'd known that she was all wrong. She had worn her brown and white saddle shoes with white bobby socks, which all the girls in her old school wore, and her tiered black skirt with the small, wine-red polka dots and her peasant blouse. But these girls wore skimpy black shoes like ballet slippers. They wore full, solid-color skirts and blouses with wide belts. She'd felt ridiculous with her clunky shoes and baby clothes. That night, she'd pulled everything out of her closet, making two piles: clothes she could wear and clothes she couldn't. The next afternoon, she'd gotten her mother to buy her a new pair of shoes, "Capezios" they were called. She stuck her saddle shoes, which she had loved, into the back of her closet.

It wasn't until three weeks after her shopping trip with Elly, when she could no longer ignore how cold it was getting, that Delia actually wore her new coat. Riding the subway to her school, she anticipated the worst (her friends saying "Oh, you have a new coat") and the best ("That's a really neat coat!"). But as she and her friends waited on the school steps, no one remarked on it. When the doors finally opened, she merged into the hallway with everyone else and rushed up the stairs. Her friend Astrid told her that Mrs. Tucci, their English teacher and a friend of Astrid's mother, wouldn't be in school that day because her husband had died over the weekend.

"I'm going to the funeral parlor after school. My

mother says Mrs. Tucci will be glad to see us. Can you come?"

Delia nodded. "I've never been to a funeral parlor, have you?"

"No. My mother says people sit quietly and talk about the person who died. She said we don't have to stay long. What matters is being there."

As she hung up her things in her locker, Delia thought how odd it was that Astrid hadn't said anything about her coat. For a split second she'd thought that Astrid was looking right at it, about to say something, but then the moment passed. Astrid was an expert on just about everything and would be right about the coat, but Delia couldn't possibly ask her what she thought.

An American flag waved high over the entrance to the funeral parlor. The entrance was imposing. They both paused. What Delia and Astrid shared more than anything was their dislike of their stepmothers and their love for their English teacher. They talked about Mrs. Tucci incessantly, quoted her, noted bits of information they learned about her, looked up her address and phone number in the phone book—for what purpose they couldn't say.

They held back for a moment.

"C'mon," Astrid finally said, striding up the steps to the front door.

A tall man in a black suit appeared, one of several men who looked just like him, moving in and out of doorways.

"Who are you looking for?"

"Our teacher, Mrs. Tucci."

"Tucci," he repeated. "Follow me." He led them noiselessly on the deep carpet down a hall and through a door into a room that Delia thought looked like someone's grandmother's living room. The man disappeared and the girls stood just inside the door, uncertain what to do next. Delia felt a wave of self-consciousness in the bright orange of her coat.

Sitting across the room with a group of people, Mrs. Tucci caught sight of them.

"Oh my goodness, my girls." She rose and came forward, put an arm around each of them. She hugged them and smiled, her eyes tearing.

"How touching, how very, very touching. Thank you for coming."

"We're sorry about your husband," Astrid said.

"Yes," Delia added, "we're very sorry."

The girls stood on either side of Mrs. Tucci, a

tall, handsome woman, her silver-streaked dark hair pulled back into a chignon. She beckoned to a young man, who rose from his chair and approached them.

"This is my son, Atilio," Mrs. Tucci said. "Atilio, these are two of my girls from American Literature. Aren't they wonderful for coming? You already know Astrid," she continued, taking Astrid's hand. Atilio leaned forward and kissed Astrid on the cheek.

"And this is Delia, our lovely new girl," she added, reaching out for Delia's hand. "Delia's hard at work on an independent project, Atilio, a very promising research paper on Walt Whitman."

She turned to Delia. "Atilio is a Whitman scholar."

"Oh!" Delia said, pleased but not sure what to say next.

"I hope I can see your paper when it's finished." Atilio smiled.

"I would be so honored," Delia said. She worried they were all running out of things to say and shifted uncomfortably beneath her coat.

"We're sorry about your dad," Astrid said, then added that Mrs. Tucci was their best teacher. Delia joined in and said that the American Literature course was the best she had ever taken.

"Oh, they flatter me," their teacher said with a

smile to her son. Then turning back to the girls, she said, "You were so good to come, I am really very touched. I'm sure that you'll be expected home soon, and I don't want you to feel that you have to stay, but we thank you so much for coming." She moved toward the door, stopping a few times to tell people who they were and how moved she was that they had come. As they reached the receiving hall, she embraced them again.

The girls waved goodbye. The man who had greeted them appeared from nowhere with a slight smile on his face and held out his arm, directing them back down the hall to the front door.

"That's quite a coat," he said to Delia as she passed him.

Once outside, Delia and Astrid caught their crosstown bus. Delia was so stricken by the man's words, she could barely pretend to listen to Astrid as they jostled against each other in their seats with the movements of the bus. What had that man meant? She was relieved when they finally got through the park and Astrid pulled the rope to signal her stop at Central Park West.

"I'll talk to you tonight after dinner," Astrid called out as she jumped off.

Delia stared, unseeing, out the bus window. It didn't matter, she told herself, about her coat. Look at what Mrs. Tucci said about her, that she was lovely and a good student. And Mrs. Tucci's son said he would like to read her paper and he sounded like he really meant it. This was what was important. Nobody stared at her. And maybe that man liked her coat. But then she pictured Astrid, tall, long-limbed, her black hair piled up on her head, her beautiful creamy skin. Everyone noticed Astrid. Astrid was perfect.

Delia wanted to be perfect, too. But sitting on the bus, she became convinced that she had made a stupid mistake, that the coat was all wrong. She couldn't wait to get out of it.

For the next few days, Delia wore an old car coat of Cassy's. She hoped her mother would notice. Then maybe she could tell her how awful she felt in her new coat. Maybe her mother would solve her problem. She knew, though, that a winter coat was a major purchase, that you couldn't just get rid of a perfectly good coat because you changed your mind.

And there was the problem of Elly. She had the feeling that Elly thought of the coat as some kind of bond between them. During the next week, when she had her weekly dinner at her father's, Elly asked about the coat. Delia said it was being shortened.

The second Wednesday in December was the day for teachers' meetings so this was a half-day. Her mother wouldn't be home for hours. Delia sat at her desk squinting at her homework assignments. But her mind kept wandering. This would be the time.

She got up and opened her closet door, pulled out the orange coat, and laid it on the bed. Spread out, it looked really nice. But she knew that the moment she put it on, she would feel hopeless in it, a girl who couldn't put herself together, a girl who even if she was smart was not one of the best girls.

As she walked down the hall to her mother's room, a noise startled her. She thought it was the key turning in the front door. But it was nothing, just the radiator in the living room. She opened her mother's closet. On her hands and knees, she rummaged on the floor behind her mother's clothes. There, among the boxes, was the large straw sewing basket that probably had not been opened since her grandmother was alive. Delia pulled it out and opened it. Lying on top of the jumble of notions was what she was looking for: a pair of heavy shears with black handles. She closed the lid and shoved the basket into its place, and brought the scissors back to her room.

She picked up the coat by the hem, on the button side, and dug the scissors in. She couldn't get them to move, so she dropped the coat and squeezed down on the handles as hard as she could; the scissors came together a bit, making a little tear, but they wouldn't budge any farther. She pushed them forward and squeezed again. This was hardly making a dent. Stymied, she stared at the coat, then remembered the box of razor blades in her medicine chest. These would work better than scissors.

When she'd finished slicing she stood back and surveyed what she had done. The gash ran several inches up the front, about two inches to the right of the buttons. The coat was rumpled, so she shook it out a little and discovered that if she pushed the edges of the slice together, no one would know it was there. Pieced together, the coat looked handsome. She admired its shape, its narrow lapels, its soft texture. Even its color. She now thought that the orange was striking in a good way. That's what the man in the funeral parlor meant.

What had possessed her to do such a stupid thing? As she hung the coat back in her closet, she was seized with regret, then panic. She had ruined it; she'd be in big trouble.

Later that night, after a dinner of beef stew and salad with her mother, after watching Perry Mason on television, talking to Astrid on the phone, working on her Whitman essay, and taking her shower in the clawfoot tub in her bathroom off her bedroom—the maid's room in the olden days of the building—and after kissing her mother goodnight, Delia turned off her light and lay on her back in bed.

The constant light of the city came through her night window in a sulphurous glow, softly illuminating the objects and furniture in her room. She heard clattering dishes, water running, muffled voices from somebody's television coming from open windows in the building across the courtyard. The sky in the city is never pitch black; it is never quiet. It was hard to get used to. Beyond her window the world was busy, indifferent; in her room, silent and small, she was anguishing over an orange coat.

She would tell her mother that someone at Jerry's Coffee Shop cut her coat where it was hanging while she was having an egg cream with her friends after school. And that no one, not Jerry or his wife or anyone, saw it happen or could figure out how it happened. A mystery.

She would tell her mother that it happened at school, that she found it in her locker, her padlock broken, slashed up the front.

She would put the coat in a garbage bag and stuff it in a trash can out on the street, somewhere not in her neighborhood, and tell her mother it was stolen. This thought stopped her dead. That was all she'd needed to do in the first place.

Nearly asleep, she jerked awake, horrified by what she'd done and frightened of being caught. Oh God, she thought, what am I going to do?

"Your father called last night after you went to bed," her mother said as they sat at the kitchen counter over cereal and banana. "He said that Elly was upset— no, that's not right—concerned—Elly is concerned you didn't wear your new coat last week or the week before when you were there for dinner. You told her it was being shortened, but she didn't think it needed shortening. She's apparently disappointed, too." Her mother paused and Delia waited.

"And then, you know, I realized that I hadn't noticed—I've been so busy—but I don't think I've seen your new coat since the first day you showed it to me. Have I? You don't wear it, do you?"

Delia shook her head.

"You don't like it, do you?" her mother said, reaching her hand across the table toward Delia.

Now was the moment, Delia thought, to tell her. But instead, bursting into tears, she said "I look stupid in it, dumpy and vulgar."

"Oh, Delia, you don't, you look lovely in it, you really do. But if you really don't like it, instead of moping around about it, why didn't you just say so? We might still be able to take it back but if we can't we can take it to that consignment store across town and then go to Best's and get you something you like."

"It's too late, Mom. I've ruined the coat."

Delia felt relief and shame as her words tumbled out—how she felt all wrong in the coat, how she didn't want to shop with Elly in the first place.

"I'm angry! Really angry and there's no one I can talk to. I can't talk to you, you're busy and you need to go to school. And I can't talk to Daddy, Elly's always there. And Cassy isn't here. I can't talk to any of you. And I don't even want to talk to Elly. And I feel like I'm so unsophisticated at school. I feel like a hick. If it wasn't for Mrs. Tucci, I'd feel like a total nobody."

When she finished, her mother looked at her

for a long time her brow tight with little lines of disapproval.

"I don't quite know what to say. I'm horrified, really I am, that you slashed your coat with a razor. What on earth did you think you were doing?" She lapsed into silence as Delia sat silently, her face wet with tears.

"I know that life isn't so easy for you right now, but I am really upset with you. We have to pay attention to this," she said. "I do, Daddy does, and you do. We need to talk about it together, and we will."

Delia kept her head down, but nodded.

"Right now, though, you need to think about what you're going to say to Elly. You'll have to figure that out for yourself, but you do understand, don't you, that you have to say something, that's she's been asking. She's done what she thought was a nice thing, a nice way to be together and you can't go on as if it never happened."

Delia did, she did understand. She promised her mother she would, she would call Elly.

The following Tuesday, after school, when her mother wasn't home, Delia sat down at the hall table in front of the telephone with the piece of composition paper on which she had written three possible versions of what to say. The third sounded best and that's what she decided to say. She dialed and got ready to read. But when Elly answered, Delia didn't refer to her notes.

"I'm sorry, Elly, about the coat," she began.

Elephants and Hawks

"Johnny is a fa-ag, Johnny is a fa-ag," David and Tommy chant in whispers as the fourth graders prance around in a large circle to the music, played on the piano by Judy Silver, whom they all call Judy.

"Now you are elephants," she calls out over the room as she bangs down chords that alternate between her right and left hand. "Swing that trunk, Sophie."

The children, some of them giggling, some of them muttering "This is baby stuff," nevertheless move around the room more or less working at following Judy's prompt.

Johnny, slim and light, seems to gain weight as he sinks into his limbs and lumbers along, suggesting the sway of a trunk with a slight but graceful movement of his arm leading him.

"Beautiful, Johnny. You *are* an elephant," Judy calls out. "Now, quick, everyone, you are hawks," she announces, changing the piano from chords to runs.

More willing to be hawks than elephants, the children immediately spread out their arms and zoom around the room, sometimes bumping into each other, flapping their hands and laughing.

Johnny spreads his arms and holds them still, slowly running and banking to one side, then another, as he circles round and round.

"Don't flap your wings, Laura," Judy calls out. "Watch what Johnny is doing. You've all seen hawks fly and circle around."

At the end of the movement class, Judy lines the children up and takes them back to their classroom.

In the back of the line, David and Tommy whisper, "Johnny is a fa-ag, Johnny is a fa-ag."

Johnny, just ahead of them, turns around and looks at them for a moment. "I don't even hear you," he says. He turns away and walks back to the classroom with the others in that funny way he has, gracefully, toes seeming to hit the floor first.

Dream House

The springer spaniel leaped forward on her leash, yanking at Cheri who tottered behind on her skimpy sandal heels.

"Damn you!" she yelled, jerking back on her leash. She brought the dog to her and started out again. Again, the dog shot forward, pulling on her leash, as they walked over the dune and onto the beach. Finally at the water's edge, the pretty liver-and-white spaniel strained first in one direction, then another, her nose to the ground. Sandpipers flew up in alarm; seagulls simply moved out of her path. Cheri pulled on the leash to no avail.

"Lily heel!"

The dog paused and looked at Cheri before jumping lightly forward, pulling Cheri after her.

A woman, approaching them, smiled and leaned over to pet Lily. Cheri noticed her thick leather sandals, her pale pink polo, her khaki shorts with the big patch pocket on the outer thigh (of all places to put a pocket!).

"What a beautiful dog." The woman rubbed Lily's ears.

"My name's Jane," she said, looking up at Cheri and offering her hand. "I believe I'm staying in the cottage next to yours, cottage number 5?"

"Uh huh. I think I noticed your arrival yesterday. Name's Cheri. This your first time?"

"It is, and I must say I feel as if I'd landed in heaven. I'm from Guilford—Guilford, Vermont? And right now it's probably ten below there."

"We're from Connecticut—Fairfield," Cheri said flashing a brilliant smile, "and I know how you feel. I have no return ticket. My husband's away—Lily! Stop pulling!"

Cheri yanked back on the stretched-out leash.

"And this, this," she repeated gesturing with her free hand, "is his dog."

"She's a beauty."

"She is, she's beautiful. But as my mother used to say, 'Beauty is as beauty does,' and this dog's impossible." Cheri shielded her eyes from the sun with the back of her hand. She frowned at Jane, who seemed to be waiting attentively for the next thing Cheri might say.

"I can't do this, I just can't. My husband went back home for a couple of weeks—work—and wouldn't take her with him. Refused. 'Just walk them together,' he said. Huh! Lily just doesn't obey and it ruins Mitzi's walk so I have to walk four times a day instead of two. She's impossible. I'm going to have to ship her off to the kennel and he's not going to like that. In fact," Cheri's voice lowered as she leaned toward Jane, "he'll kill me. But this is all his fault. He insisted on getting another dog. Mitzi's six and she's always been mine really, bonded to me from the start. A bichon. Perfectly behaved. You'll see her, she's adorable," Cheri flashed her smile again. "So I said 'fine you get another dog and she'll be your dog.' I didn't want another dog, but he did so here we are. But I can't do this." She gestured toward Lily, who was sniffing at Jane's feet. "I really can't. This is impossible." She looked out at the water.

The day was brilliant. The blue water was ruffled with an occasional whitecap in the distance. The few clouds had sharp edges. Cheri's hair shone gold against her tanned face. Her eyes, rimmed with black eyeliner, took in Jane's calm face, framed by unruly red curls. Cheri stood for a moment longer, silent, her black miniskirt lifting in the breeze, then shrugged and moved on, the dog pulling ahead.

"You're just not used to her," Jane called after her. "You'll get used to each other and it'll be fine."

"You think?" Cheri said, glancing back.

Don had already stopped at the kennel to collect Lily before he pulled up to cottage number 6 in his VW convertible. He stepped out and opened the passenger door. Lily remained sitting on the back seat, eager but restrained, as he lifted out his suitcase. He looked at her.

"Okay!"

The dog bounded out of the car and started for the beach, just beyond their cottage. Don whistled and she spun around, racing back to his side, ears flopping. She sat, looking up at him.

He was a man of medium height and build with plenty of reddish, brown hair shot through with gray. He sported a thick, somewhat disheveled mustache over his unsmiling mouth. He looked at Lily.

"Okay," he said, and together, he and Lily mounted the steps to the cottage.

Don found Cheri in the sitting room watching an Oprah rerun on the huge flat screen built into the wall. Cheri had the air conditioner running full blast although it wasn't that hot outside. She'd closed the blinds against the late afternoon sun; it took a moment for his eyes to adjust. Mitzi was a curly white ball in Cheri's lap.

Don bent over Cheri's chair and kissed her on the cheek. "Well, Lily isn't any the worse for wear. The kennel people said she was fine, happy even, with the other dogs." He frowned. "Lucky for you is all I'll say."

"I told you it would be all right," Cheri said, not taking her eyes off the TV screen.

"You seem thrilled to see me."

"I'm watching this. It'll be over in a minute."

Don went back to the kitchen. He called to Cheri from the bar as he took down an Old Fashioned glass and poured his drink over a handful of ice cubes.

"You want a drink?"

"Not right now."

He leaned down and stroked Lily under her ear, shook the ice cubes back and forth in his glass, and moved into the sitting room, Lily at his heels. As he passed Cheri, he reached out and tousled Mitzi's head and Mitzi, excited, leapt down and stood at his feet bouncing up and down at his ankles.

"Wha'dya do that for?" Cheri said. "Put her back on my lap. If you want to pet someone, pet Lily."

Don plopped Mitzi back on Cheri's lap, placed his drink on the floor, and lay down on his back beside it. Lily stretched herself out by his head and panted.

"Your back hurting again?"

"Yeah. It's the driving. After half an hour I get this pain in my butt and down the outside of my leg. I may have to get a new car down here. I just can't make the VW comfortable. I never have this trouble in the Audi."

They lapsed into silence. Oprah's voice alternated with her guest's as she asked him probing questions.

"Any time you're finished," Don said, staring at the ceiling. "I'm ready to go to dinner."

"This is almost over," she said.

Don liked its darkness, the big golden oak bar, the oak booths of Doc Ford's, a noisy restaurant, patronized mostly by winter visitors and half-year residents like themselves. He liked the high-mounted TVs flashing images of shiny cars, rolling golf courses, exotic birds, exploding buildings in faraway places, the sounds drowned out by the chatter and laughter of people having a good time. Best ribs on the island. He ordered another Old Fashioned and Cheri ordered a glass of Chardonnay. Cheri's thick blonde hair wasn't her real color but he found it stunning, piled casually on her head like that. In the dim light, her white teeth gleamed against her deep red, almost black lipstick and dusky face as she talked and laughed. She seemed nakedly plump in her skimpy black top. She was stupid about the dogs—maddening—but right now, sitting across from her, all he could think about was getting into bed with her.

"What're you having?" he asked.

"I think I'll have the 'peel and eat' shrimp and a house salad."

"Fine. I'm having the ribs. Another wine?"

"Why not?"

He ordered and they sat in silence.

"I showed the cottage to a couple from Akron, Ohio this week," she said.

"How'd it go?"

"They're not going to buy it. They were shocked by the price. I told them it was just renovated. They thought it was over-decorated."

She shrugged. "They were pretty blunt, I guess you would say."

She leaned forward, accentuating her cleavage.

"And I heard them talking when they thought I was out of hearing. They didn't like the dark furniture, and the dark floors and rugs in a white beach cottage. They thought it should be light and white inside too."

"Isn't it funny that they seem to have said exactly what you said when we were redoing it?"

"Well, they said it with no help from me. And they thought seven hundred thousand was outrageous;

I heard them talking in the kitchen. Outrageous."

"And what did you say?"

"Not a thing. I didn't think it was proper for me to comment."

"This sounds suspiciously like 'I told you so' to me," Don said. "I say fuck them. Seven hundred thousand for a cottage on the beach in the best part of southwestern Florida doesn't sound like too much to me. If we're going to buy that condo, we damn well better get a good price for the cottage. Unless you've decided you don't care about having the condo?"

"Who said anything like that?" Cheri said.

"Well, now that I'm here, I'll take buyers around. We want to sell this place."

"Whatever," Cheri said.

As he gnawed on a rib, Don looked across the table at her and felt his desire drain away.

"Hey Cheri, hi!"

Don peered in the direction of the voice.

A woman with unruly hair was approaching their table. She was wearing some god-awful combination of baggy clothes.

Cheri looked up and smiled. "This is our neighbor in cottage number 5 and she thinks Lily is beautiful," she said to her husband.

"And this is my husband, Don, who thinks Lily is beautiful, too," Cheri added, giving a little laugh.

"The name's Jane," Jane said. "Nice to meet you."

"Same here," Don said, not smiling.

Jane looked around. "This place feels a lot more local than other restaurants I've been to, not that I've been to that many. I've heard the ribs here are outstanding."

"We're about finished," Cheri said. Then, afraid that she had seemed rude, added, "But why don't you sit down for a minute while we have our coffee."

"Oh thanks, maybe I will. I'm meeting a friend, but I'm a little early."

Cheri made room for Jane on her side of the booth.

"It must be so nice to get back here," Jane said to Don, "after having to interrupt your vacation and go back to work."

"I don't mind going back and forth."

"Um, what is your work?"

"I own a software company that manages medical databases."

"He started the company from nothing," Cheri said.

"Interesting," Jane said, leaning forward.

"Important, too, I should say. I mean hospital data. What a huge responsibility!"

Cheri glanced at Don who was staring into his empty glass. He was checking out.

"And what about you?" she said, turning to Jane. "What do you do?"

"I teach writing to incoming freshmen at a community college. I started out as an editor, but found my way into teaching along the way. You have no idea how possible it is for really bright students to be so dismal in language skills. It's always a little overwhelming at the beginning of the year but then they get better and better. I love it."

Cheri looked at Jane, her curly red hair, her lightly freckled face. She was actually kind of pretty, prettier than her clothes.

"That certainly sounds like important work, too," Cheri said. "A hundred years ago, I thought I was going to teach, but life went in a different direction." She looked again at Don, who shifted in his seat.

"Will you ladies excuse me?" Don said. "Nature calls."

Later, as he and Cheri were leaving the restaurant, he said, "Where the hell did you find her?"

"I didn't find her, she's our neighbor."

"Well, I hope she's not going to become a presence in our lives."

"I don't know. She's all right." Cheri paused. "In fact, I rather like her."

"What the hell do you like about her?"

Cheri spread out her right hand and contemplated her blackish-red fingernails, painted to go with her lipstick.

"I think I like her because she's not like us," she said.

When Cheri woke up, the sun was hard up against the blinds. She could feel the brightness outside. She turned on her back. Don was already up and gone. She lifted her head. Lily was lying on the floor at the foot of the bed. Mitzi jumped up and down against Cheri's side, making her little barking noises. Cheri swooped down and picked her up, settling her on her stomach.

"Honey, honey," she crooned. "Did you have a good sleep?" Mitzi cocked her head as if she was listening for particular words.

"Hungry, honey?" Cheri rubbed her head roughly.

Mitzi scrambled around on the king-sized bed, barking.

"Okay, okay."

Cheri pushed back the duvet and swung her legs off the bed, catching her feet in the gold slippers awaiting her on the floor. She pulled on a black satin robe and went down the hall, Mitzi and Lily at her heels. She poured from the bag of dog food on the kitchen counter into Mitzi's white ironstone dish, then placed it on the floor.

"Here's your breakfast, honey."

She put a few kibbles into Lily's dish, too, knowing that Don would have fed and walked her already.

Don had made the coffee and put it in the carafe. She poured herself a cup, sat on the pale birch barstool at the counter and sipped as she looked out at the bright day, at the wild beach grape, visible from the kitchen window, scrabbling over the dunes. Mitzi and Lily sat at the foot of the stool, looking up.

"You're not getting a thing."

Cheri toasted an English muffin and downed a glass of orange juice. She got a plate, spoon, and pot of jam and sat down again. The two dogs sat like statues at her feet.

When she and Don first bought the cottage, she had envisioned lightness: pale wood floors, cherry cabinets and white walls, puffy down pillows in beige slipcovers on the sofa, old-fashioned white ironstone china—light, everything light, airy, a feeling of outside inside. She had loved it, her vision for it, her dream house. She looked now at the marble countertops, the overstuffed chairs covered with chocolate leather, at the freshly refinished floors, stained dark brown, covered with Orientals in red, orange, and brown. Admittedly beautiful but not light and beachy. It all went together but it was too heavy, too heavy for a white cottage on the beach. That was a big fight, fifteen years ago, one of their biggest. But he was in charge, the expert on interior design, he made all the decisions, and by now, she thought looking around, did she care? They were going to sell it. Someone was going to buy it. For seven hundred, six fifty, six. For a lot.

She picked up the remote and switched on the TV. The screen wavered, then sprang to life, catching men and women racing down a dusty street, their clothes flapping, unaware, totally unaware that they were being watched by thousands, no millions, of people. A parked car exploded, debris shot up in the air and fell everywhere. Anguished bloody faces filled the screen. The announcer shouted over the noise of screaming. A line of unrelated words paraded across the bottom of the screen. How awful, she thought, how awful, awful. But what could you do? She snapped the TV off.

Reveling in her solitude, she stretched, pulled the muffin out of the toaster, and slathered one half with plum jam, leaving the other half dry. Well, she was lucky in one way: he was either in Fairfield or running around all over the island on errands and projects. She wondered where he was this morning.

No matter, today she would walk Mitzi and read her book in the chair outside the cottage, maybe go to the beach in the afternoon and have a nice long conversation on her cell with Charlotte back home. She'd skip lunch; he'd want to go out for a big dinner tonight.

Mitzi gave a little yelp.

"Oh, I'm sorry. I forgot, honey. Here." And she tore a small piece of the English muffin and reached down to Mitzi, who eagerly snatched it up. She broke up the rest of it into many pieces and gave Mitzi another piece. She glanced at Lily, who was sitting at attention; Cheri leaned over and gave her a hunk of the muffin.

"Dammit, Cheri, I've told you I don't want you

feeding Lily from the table," Don's voice boomed into the room. "You can do what you want with Mitzi, but don't spoil Lily."

Cheri started.

"Well, I can't exactly just give Mitzi treats when Lily is sitting there. That's mean."

"They're dogs, Cheri, not your children. And anyway, how about not feeding Mitzi, either. Bread isn't good for them."

"Why don't you get a life?"

"What's that supposed to mean?"

"What difference does it make if I give Lily a treat every once in a while? Why make a thing of it?"

"Because you don't think about these things. You think everything is unimportant. So I have to…"

"Let's talk about something else," Cheri held the palm of her hand out in a stop position. "Where were you this morning?"

"Aha!" Don seemed happy to move on. "I went out to Fort Myers to check out an antiques show. I bought something." As he smiled, his mustache moved with his mouth and his blue eyes crinkled.

"What? What did you buy?"

"Guess."

"Oh c'mon, honey, how would I know? A

painting?"

"No."

"Just tell me, tell me what you bought."

"I got a marquetry table for the front hall at home. It's in perfect condition. Eighteenth century, exquisite. Here, I took a picture." He took his digital camera out of his khaki vest pocket and turned it on.

"Here, look," he walked over and leaned on the counter close to her and they both looked at the tiny picture.

"It's gorgeous," Cheri said, feeling his body through her robe. She considered for a moment leaning into him, but didn't. "It will look really good there. How much?"

"Four thousand."

"Hmmm."

"You like it?"

"It's gorgeous," Cheri repeated.

Don straightened up and sat on the stool opposite Cheri. "I thought you might like it."

"Then I went to the realtors," he continued. "Jim said that he didn't expect you to be here when he came with those buyers this week. He called to warn you and expected you to let them in and then leave."

"Nice of him to tell me."

"He said he did. It's not a good idea to have the owners around when you show a house, Cheri. You know that."

"Well, he didn't ask me to leave."

"I'm sure he didn't want to be rude. But he'd like me to be here from now on."

"So it's all right if you're here?"

"Ah, but I know the drill," Don said. "It's all about selling, Cheri. Every buyer says the asking price of a house is outrageous. You don't pay any attention. It's part of the dance."

"Fine," Cheri said. "If it sells the cottage, you do the dance." She kicked out her legs and then hooked them back onto the rung of her stool.

"Then I went out to the east end to look at the condo again," Don said, ignoring her. "It's empty now. I made an appointment with the realtor. I'm going to make my move. They'll come down in price, I'm sure of it. Probably by fifty thousand. Course, we'd buy it for the asking price, but they don't have to know that. I spent a lot of time there this time. Great space. Everything updated, built in. And the view of the ocean from the balcony is spectacular. It's got everything we've got at home. You serious about wanting to stay until April? You'd be very comfortable.

Makes this place look like a slum."

"I'm ready," Cheri said, gazing across the room through the window at the dune rising to the beach. "I loved it. It's a dream come true." She got up and went back to the bedroom, Mitzi at her heels.

Cheri sat on the white Adirondack chair outside her cottage. She wore her black bathing suit, gold-rimmed granny sunglasses, and her hair back with a pink chiffon scarf. She balanced a book in her lap—a John Grisham—but she wasn't reading. She looked out on the familiar grassy dune, at the dip the path cut through it, out to the water's edge, at the triangle of blue-green water. Mitzi sat inside the house at the screen door watching the world go by.

Although Cheri was enjoying her book, she didn't feel like reading just now. She was thinking about Don, about how she liked it better when he was away. Maybe the best part about being down here was the fact that he could never stay for more than two or three weeks in a row. She loved having so much time to herself.

"Hi there, Cheri."

Cheri looked up, a ready smile on her face. Standing in front of her was—what *was* her name?

Her neighbor in the clunky sandals and awful khaki shorts. "Oh, hi."

"It's Jane," the neighbor said, laughing in recognition of Cheri's predicament. "Great day, isn't it?"

"Jane, right," Cheri said, smiling. "Just a momentary lapse. Yes, a perfect day."

"Were you by any chance at the dance concert last night?...No? It was fabulous. Do you like dance?"

"I guess I can take it or leave it."

"Well I'm an aficionado—I guess I should say aficionada—and this was really good. Seems like there's a lot of good things to do down here."

Jane paused. "I saw Don on the beach with Lily this morning."

"You must have been up with the birds," Cheri said.

"It was pretty early. Lily sure paid attention to him."

"Tell me about it."

"You know, I think dogs respond better to men anyway. The alpha voice and all. But I was thinking. You should get a halti collar. You know about those? They go over the dog's nose and they imitate some discipline gesture mother dogs make, so it sort of speaks to the dog. Anyway, when they have the halti on they get a correction on their noses if they lunge forward. It's not painful or anything. I have a friend who uses it with her Portuguese water dog, a real handful. It really works. You should try it."

"Hmmm. I'll have to look into it," Cheri said, opening her book.

Jane didn't move. "I hear your cottage is for sale?"

"Yup."

"But someone said you just renovated it; what a shame not to stay in it after all that work. I must say from here it looks so gorgeous."

"We did put in a lot of effort, but we got an opportunity to buy a condo on East Drive in a small four-story building with all the extras: a pool, concierge services, beautiful grounds." Cheri closed her book. "Not scruffy like this. The one we're interested in is on the second floor with a view of the ocean. It's super. This cottage is great, but the condo is more to our liking. And I'm thinking of staying here for the whole winter, you know, November to April, and Don can come back and forth every couple of weeks or so. So the condo makes much more sense."

Why was she going on like this, Cheri thought.

Why did she want this earnest woman to understand all her reasoning about the cottage? But she couldn't stop.

"Don has to be at his company a lot of the time, but he makes his own time and anyway, he buys and sells antiques kind of as a hobby and likes to be up there for shows. And I love it here. I have no reason to be there all the time. I mean, I have girlfriends and all, but I can invite them down here and anyway they all go away in the winter, too. So if I'm going to stay here all winter, I want something, well, something better than a white cottage on the beach."

"Well, I guess I can see that, but I like these cottages. So simple, no fuss. Light and spare, like the beach. A cottage like any one of these is my idea of perfect. If I could afford it I would grab yours in a minute. Fact is, renting one for two weeks is a big extravagance for me."

What a gross thing to say out loud, Cheri thought, embarrassed for Jane.

"You know what?" she said, leaning toward Jane, "I actually would love to hand it over, I really would. But of course I can't."

She sat back. "Are you married?"

"No."

"Ever been?"

"Well, no, not married."

"You're lucky."

"You don't really mean that!" Jane gave a tentative laugh.

"You're shocked?"

"Not shocked. Well, maybe a little. More surprised, I guess, that you would say that to me, practically a stranger. Seems sort of, well, disloyal."

"I don't know. I don't see what loyalty has to do with it. See, if I weren't married, I could seriously consider just giving you the cottage or selling it for much, much less than we're asking. I really could. Or I could invite you to dinner without worrying that Don might not like you, would find you boring, would be rude and excuse himself the minute dinner was over and disappear into his computer. Look." Cheri leaned forward as if to divulge a secret. "Listen, what could you afford for a cottage?"

"Oh, don't be silly, I mean, I don't know, I couldn't afford it. That's all I know." Jane seemed flustered.

"No, I really mean it. Let's just imagine. What could you possibly, possibly afford?"

"Well, okay. Fifty thousand? I wouldn't want to

touch my retirement funds."

Cheri sat back in her chair. "Here's what I mean about you being lucky. We could afford to sell this cottage to you for fifty thousand. Easily. And, you know, I think I would actually do it. It would be a great thing to do. But Don wouldn't. Don would really think I was insane or retarded. If I weren't married, I would be free, like you. That's what I mean about being lucky."

"Well, sure, you're constrained in certain ways, I'm sure, but then there are the good parts about being married, the companionship, doing things together, physical closeness—not just sex, but touching. Not being lonely."

"That's what you imagine because you don't have it, but really, marriage can be very lonely. Marriage is as much a burden as a joy. In fact, a joy is what it isn't." She dropped her book into a basket by her chair.

"So why do you stay with him?"

Cheri looked at Jane, at her open, questioning face, then looked beyond her at the triangle of blue water caught between the dunes.

"I can't imagine life without him," she said.

In the sitting room Don sprawled in his slatted chair opposite the TV, his legs splayed out, one hand grazing the floor, kneading Lily's ear, the other holding the remote. He clicked and clicked again as images barely taken in flashed by like landscape on a train. He lingered when the sight of men and guns and smoke—signs of war—caught his attention. Vietnam, he judged, from the landscape, the attire. A familiar narrating voice oozed from the speakers and Don settled in. A PBS history special. His mind wandered. He thought about his father, a World War II veteran. Never talked about it much except to say that he had been proud to serve his country. Don was drafted during Vietnam but never left Fort Dix. Luck of the draw. Met Cheri. Sister of his buddy at Fort Dix. Fell head over heels. Had to have her. And now, twenty-five years later, she could still turn him on.

Cheri had gotten into bed early, piling three pillows behind her, leaning back, her knees up supporting her book and Mitzi burrowing under the blankets. She could hear the TV from the sitting room where Don was watching a war special. Cheri knew nothing about war, any war, even though she had studied nothing but wars in her high school history classes.

High school. Her parents divorced and suddenly there was no money, so they took her out of her fancy private school in New York, took her away from her friends, and sent her across town to Mary Peabody, the huge public high school, all girls, six thousand of them, lots of blacks, Hispanics, bad English, big fistfights in the cafeteria. Class of '65. Horrible. The memory of hundreds of girls wearing their school hats with MPHS in blue written on the brims, sitting in the cafeteria, screaming and yelling and eating the hideous-smelling food. You didn't want to bump into them in the girls' room. Some of them were dangerous. She'd had one friend, Priscilla, a black girl—whatever happened to her?—but mostly she'd kept to herself and gotten by, kept out of trouble, gotten her diploma and put the whole experience out of her mind. She went to the State University and majored in education. She'd thought she might as well teach. She didn't know what else there was and she liked children. She sat in the cafeteria with all the other Ed. majors, tootling nursery songs on their plastic recorders, wishing, wishing she were at the table across the way where the smart people, the handsome people sat. In her junior year her brother introduced her to his buddy at Fort Dix, Don. Gorgeous, solid, muscular, strong, and out of her league Don. He moved like a bear, with a graceful heaviness. She especially loved his slightly untidy reddish-brown mustache and his light, confident smile. He'd already been to Harvard Business School and as soon as his time was up he was poised to join a business in Cambridge that organized medical records for hospitals. He loved antiques; he came from a well-to-do family. He fell head over heels for Cheri. She quit school and they got married. She had lucked out.

"Hey Cheri, why don't you come on out here. Get me a drink. Have a glass of wine," Don called out as the soldiers elbowed their bodies across muddy ground in the dark.

Cheri appeared in the bedroom door in her black dressing gown and gold slippers.

He grinned.

"Whad'llya have?" she asked, leaning against the doorframe.

"Bourbon and ice," he said, looking back at the screen.

Cheri moved past him and through to the kitchen. She poured him three inches of bourbon over sharp, square ice cubes and poured herself a glass of wine. She walked back to the sitting room and stood before him, handing him the glass.

"Sit on me," he said, looking up at her.

And she did, straddling him in his chair.

As their bodies found each other she said to herself, as she often did, I hate you Don, hate you from the bottom of my heart, like a prayer or incantation, before she melted and let him in.

Behind her the TV flickered. Beside them Mitzi and Lily lay flat on the floor, waiting.

"One Kiss My Bonnie Sweetheart"

"Doesn't Laura look like she got all dressed up for today? That stupid bow in her hair?"

Laura, from the front of the class, recites Part One of "The Highwayman" by Alfred Noyes, the longest poem anyone in the class has undertaken so far.

> The wind was a torrent of darkness among
>   the gusty trees,
> The moon was a ghostly galleon toss'd upon
>   cloudy seas,
> The road was a ribbon of moonlight over the
>   purple moor,
> The highwayman came riding, riding, riding
> The highwayman came riding up to the old
>   inn door.

Now in the seventh grade, they are expected to memorize and recite poems each week.

Sophie stares at Claudia, at her long, horsey face, her ruddy cheeks, her big teeth covered with wires, her high glossy forehead and bug eyes. She shrugs and looks back at Laura.

> And dark in the dark old inn yard
> A stable creaked...

Laura touches the ribbon in her hair and looks down at her paper. She corrects herself.

"A stable wicket creaked..."

Claudia leans toward Sophie again.

" I think she picked a long one to show off, don't

you?"

"Well, I'm doing 'If' by Rudyard Kipling next week. It's just as long as Laura's. It's hard, but it's fun."

Claudia sinks back in her chair.

"One kiss my bonnie sweetheart…"

Laura reddens and smiles.

"Did you know that Laura is half Jewish?" Claudia whispers, leaning toward Sophie again, her hand cupping her mouth.

Sophie turns and stares at Claudia.

"Sooooo?"

"Well…well…you just wouldn't know it, would you?" Claudia sits back in her seat, abruptly, and folds her arms across her chest.

"Whoever is whispering will you please be quiet and respect your classmates," Mrs. Ferguson calls out.

    … he tugged at his rein in the moonlight,
and galloped away to the west.

Laura delivers the last line of Part One with a smile as her classmates begin to clap. She touches her ribbon again, then walks down between the first and second rows to her seat behind Sophie. Sophie twists around in her seat.

"That was *so* good," she says.

Nothing Brave Here

He never really understood Delia, his second daughter. That was his thought upon awakening. Even when she was a small, impish thing, she stiffened when he hugged her and, when released, flew off like a startled bird, opening a distance between them. At some point before he moved out—was she eleven, twelve?—he stopped really hugging her. He pecked her on the cheek instead, or hugged her lightly, with one arm. Something about her very existence seemed to point out his inadequacies. With Cassy, his first-born, it was different, closer and warmer. Delia had never really told him anything about herself, her doings. Now he had to wonder: Had he asked her? Was it that she didn't tell him, or had he not asked her?

He sighed. Too late now.

He yawned and stretched carefully, so as not to wake Elly. She took good care of him, this younger, second wife of his. The least he could do was let her sleep. He felt the soreness in his muscles, always there now, because, he supposed, he was old. Andrew Rienzi, seventy-eight, professor emeritus, Metaphysical Poetry, New York University. An old man. He eased himself out of bed, ran his fingers through ragged white hair, and padded softly out of the room.

The coffee, timed for 7:30, dripped into the carafe, suffusing the kitchen with its fragrance. He slid onto the stool at the counter and watched it finish its drip. As he filled his Public Radio mug, all he could think of was Delia. Delia had cancer again. First, four years ago, in her breast. Now in her bones, her liver. She was dying.

Almost nine months ago, it was Cassy, not Delia, who'd called him.

"Delia asked me to call. She didn't want to deliver this bad news again. I already called Mummy, so she knows."

So Karen already knew, Andrew thought. Then, aloud, "Hmmm?"

"Dad?...I'm sorry. I'm sorry for us all."

Andrew didn't know what to say.

"No more treatments?"

"Dr. Castle says no."

"How is she?"

"Brave, I think. But kind of blaming herself as if she has failed us. She did say at one point, 'Why is this happening to me?' And you know what I thought? I thought, 'Instead of me,' for instance."

"Or me," Andrew had said. "Why not me, an old guy?"

He sipped his coffee, remembering. He dug his fingernails into a navel orange sitting in the blue bowl and began to peel it. Why not him? The certainty that Delia was going to die ahead of him kept catching him unawares, stopped him with shock and grief. He didn't wish he could die instead of her; he just wanted her to live. He pulled an orange wedge from its neighbor, bit down on it, and savored the bracing citrus taste.

When Delia was fourteen—1950, the year the girls and their mother moved to New York from Connecticut—she'd taken up the guitar. She and her high school friends gathered in Washington Square Park, played and sang union songs, Red Army Chorus songs, and songs from the Spanish Civil War, about which they knew almost nothing. (He did remember giving Delia a book, some poetry, about the war.) Suddenly she had a guitar that someone had given her—had she asked him for one? Why hadn't she?— and she began to teach herself to play. She was a natural. Unlike Cassy, Delia had loved her piano lessons, but there hadn't been room for a piano in the New York apartment so she'd had to give them up. How disappointing that must have been, he now thought.

So instead, she sang and strummed on the guitar with her friends. (Why hadn't she taken guitar lessons?) Once when they'd sat in the living room together, just the two of them at dusk, she'd begun to strum and sing one of his favorite labor movement songs—about the great union leader:

> I dreamed I saw Joe Hill last night
> Alive as you and me
> Says I "But Joe you're ten-years dead"
> "I never died" says he
> "I never died" says he.

As he'd listened in that darkening room, he suddenly realized that his face was wet with tears, as his face was now, remembering. That was forty years ago. Forty years.

Elly arrived in the kitchen in her white terry dressing gown. At fifty-eight she was rounded in hips and stomach, a little sloppy but pleasant-looking. Her frizzy gray curls looked the same whether combed or not. She had a beak of a nose that she had probably hated at some time, which Andrew thought was quite handsome on her broad, olive-toned face. She put her hand on his thigh.

"You look tired, hon."

"Hmm." He patted her hand.

"Breakfast?" She didn't wait for an answer, but

moved past the counter to the stove. "Isn't it tonight that you're going to stay with Delia?" She put the bread into the toaster and began to make the scrambled eggs.

"By God you're right! I had forgotten. Well, perhaps not forgotten. I woke up this morning thinking about Delia, memories…"

"Would you like me to come with you, hon? I'd be glad to."

In truth, he would. In case something happened and he didn't know what to do. He depended on Elly for so many things, he felt lost without her.

"She might like to have you to herself, but I would come if you wanted me to."

"No…thanks but no. I'll go by myself." He didn't want any of them—not Delia, or Lucy, or Cassy—to think that he was not up to this. Elly kissed his head as she put his eggs down in front of him.

After breakfast Andrew started out on his morning walk to the newsstand on Broadway, anxious about the evening ahead. Lucy, Delia's partner, who was doing her editorial work at home much of the time now, had to be out for a sales meeting. If he could come around six, she had said.

"You don't mind, Andrew, my asking you this?"

"Of course not. I want to come." And he did. Despite a feeling of discomfort, of its having been so long since he had ministered to anyone beyond bringing coffee to Elly most mornings. Despite his fear of Delia's cancer, terrible and mysterious.

He remembered sitting on the edge of Delia's bed in the dark when she'd been a little girl, feverish with tonsillitis. He'd spooned that viscous, ill-smelling and apparently bad-tasting medicine into her mouth, singing a song to distract her. He recited her favorite poems until she fell asleep. She loved anything from *Alice in Wonderland*. Did she still remember, as he did, those times together? Maybe he would ask her.

Would he sit on the edge of her bed as Cassy did, as her friends did? Would they talk? He had been to see her many times with Cassy and her husband, with Elly of course, and with Delia's closest friends, who came and went, bringing something to eat for Lucy and sitting in chairs around Delia's bed reminiscing, gossiping, laughing, weeping. Once, when her oldest friend held her hand and intoned the names of all the people who loved her—friends, family, children she had taught, their parents, colleagues—on and on like a lullaby, Delia had said, "I'd rather be alive."

Andrew looked up with a start. He had walked blocks

past the newsstand. He had a feeling that he had been talking to himself, as Elly often said he did. He turned around and retraced his steps.

Dan was standing in his place, behind the display of papers and magazines, holding out the *Times*, ready for Andrew.

"You must have something on your mind, Professor, the way you went whizzing by here."

"Thanks, Dan," Andrew said, smiling, taking the newspaper from him and dropping change into his hand. "Yes, I guess I do," he added.

Paper under his arm, Andrew walked south on Broadway back down to Seventy-Ninth Street. As he reached West End Avenue he looked down the hill past Riverside Drive. A sunny day. Ahead, beyond the park, the Hudson sparkled with whitecaps. But Andrew was not a noticing man. He looked without seeing. He stood for a moment, thinking about how the girls, already adolescents when they moved to New York, teased him. What were they always laughing at? When he asked they'd just laughed harder.

"Do you notice anything different about Delia?" Cassy once asked him when they were visiting.

Andrew peered at Delia. He thought she looked different, but couldn't tell why.

"You have eye makeup on," he ventured.

"Oh Daddy," Cassy laughed, "you're impossible! Delia's had her hair cut."

Andrew stared. Oh my God yes. Her hair, which had been shoulder-length, was now a wavy cap on her head, reaching only to her earlobes.

"It looks really nice," Andrew said, and it did, but Delia avoided his look, as if she were the one embarrassed, and it was her silence, not Cassy's words, that made him feel bad.

Andrew mounted the steps to his building and let himself in. The super was mopping the lobby floor with a dingy string mop.

"Morning, Mr. Rienzi."

Andrew threw up his hand in absentminded salute.

Elly wasn't home, he could tell, but he called out to her just the same. He went to his office, in the back of the apartment, sat in his chair, feet propped up on his desk, his *Times* in his lap. Elly wanted him to call his office his "study" but it never took.

His father had an office—"The Office," a serious place, off limits to him and his five siblings—behind the kitchen in the sprawling house in which they had grown up; but his father, a businessman, did very different things in his office than Andrew in his.

"I got my education at the Millwood Shoe Factory," his father often told his children. In his white shirtsleeves and fine woolen vest, moving back, forth, and sideways in the heavy oak chair on wheels, he'd loved to regale them with the stories of how he had taken his father's stone-masonry business and gradually transformed it into a large construction firm. Andrew's mother often proudly said that she had married a very fine man. Indeed, everyone loved him. He was generous with his time and money, was a town selectman for fifteen years, a Good Government Republican, but earthy, too, relishing a good joke, good food, Italian opera. To Andrew it seemed from his earliest childhood that he was the only one not quite in this admired man's orbit. Andrew was bookish, a day dreamer, without a head for business, lapsed in his religious upbringing, a Democrat, the one who moved away to the big city. Often, he and his father had nothing to say to each other.

Long after their father's death at age sixty-five, Andrew's sister found a journal he'd kept of his sojourn in Italy, to the Northern village where he'd been born. The vividness and poetic language of the writing surprised Andrew, left him with the feeling that somehow he had missed who his father— always practical, conscientious, successful, always the immigrant with broken English—really was.

Andrew rolled back in his chair and swung his legs to the floor. He might as well get some work done. He had been working for years on a book, a study of the Metaphysical Poets. He looked over what he had written the day before. He was pleased.

He heard the front door open and close. Elly was home. He was glad to swivel round in his chair, to leave his desk and thoughts behind (it was so unlike him, this raking over the past) and return to the kitchen where Elly was putting things away.

"You been working?"

"Yeah. A little."

"You hungry?"

"I could eat." Andrew slid onto the stool.

"How about some nice bread and cheese and fruit? We've got some MacCouns here."

Andrew nodded.

Elly prepared their lunch, moving about in the kitchen in that sure way she had, the captain of her ship.

"Did I ever tell you the story of Delia and Mary O'Hara?"

"Yes, darling, but tell it again. It's a good story."

"Karen told it one day when I came home from work. She was inside cleaning the front windows and Delia, age five or maybe six, was sitting outside on the little stone wall in front of our first house. Mary O'Hara came by to drop in on Karen, something she was always doing. She taught French in the high school and really looked the part," Andrew said, smiling, warming to the story. "She was as skinny as a child's stick figure, had a round, red face, and fluffy, shapeless hair, beige, like…like the efflorescence of smoke trees, if you know what they look like. Exactly like that, come to think of it. She was an old maid. I get to say that," Andrew cast a sheepish glance in Elly's direction, "because this was 1941 and in 1941 that's what she was. Delia didn't like Mary O'Hara. She never said so, but we all knew that Delia did not like Mary. Even Mary knew it, I feel sure, and that made her try too hard. Anyway, Mary came along—Karen saw and heard everything—passing where Delia was sitting on the wall, dangling her legs.

'Why hello there Delia,' Mary chirped (because that's what Mary did). 'I'll bet you would love an ice cream cone. Wouldn't you? Here,' she dug into her pocketbook, 'here's a nickel.'

"Karen said there was a long, long silence.

"Then, the clear, childish voice: 'If I take the nickel, do I have to like you?'"

Elly squeezed his hand. How sad he was, she thought, how sad and preoccupied. No matter what, though, he talked easily, didn't struggle for words, they just tumbled out of him in these well-wrought sentences that grew into stories, amusing stories, interesting stories, something Elly envied because she knew that she wasn't interesting. Everything in his life eventually became a story. The girls got that from him. The three of them—great storytellers. Somehow though, Andrew held himself back. He never seemed to say something unformed, something unintended, revealing. How could one so forthcoming, so engaging, be so opaque at the same time? She was used to it by now, had given up any expectation of filling in the blanks. She still had bouts of fury when living with him seemed like living alone. If she yelled at Andrew, though, he received her rage with a look of bafflement. That bafflement was an extension of what enraged her, but eventually, as he made his apologies, berated himself for his failures, she would be able to bring herself back to her equilibrium.

They ate their lunch in silence.

Just before six o'clock, as the sun was sinking across the Hudson behind New Jersey, Andrew started out on the short walk to Delia's. Lucy and Delia lived just south of him in a sprawling prewar apartment, similar to but bigger than his and Elly's. They had full work lives: Delia, headmistress, now on leave, of a private elementary school and Lucy, a book editor. He hadn't been surprised when Delia didn't get married. He was even a little relieved, given the fact that the occasional suitor she introduced to the family seemed, not a one of them, suitable at all. The last not even smart. Then no one for several years and then Lucy, with whom she got an apartment. He was glad that Delia had a roommate, didn't live alone any more, and he liked Lucy. So when Delia, after five years, told him that she and Lucy were having something called a commitment ceremony, which Elly explained to him, Andrew was happy for her, was delighted to be invited, but had to say to himself for the first time that Delia was a lesbian. It was okay in this day and age and it made some kind of sense about Delia, but it had never occurred to him before. He had never given it a thought. Elly had known it all along, thought he did, too, but somehow the subject had never come up.

Andrew reached Delia's building. He greeted the mournful doorman, took the elevator to the tenth floor in silence broken only by the occasional sound of chains jangling together in the elevator shaft.

"How're you doing?" Andrew asked.

"I'm exhausted, you know, exhausted but completely energized. But I'm okay, really. She was very chatty today, needed less morphine. And Dr. Castle came. He comes by every four or five days, talks with her about her life and about dying and he tapes it and she listens to it later. Their talks are the center of her life now. He's an amazing man. He told me once, years ago when I complained that he wasn't taking my symptoms seriously, that when a big-time illness came along I'd have his undivided attention and so would everyone who loves me. He said the most important thing a doctor does is help people to have good deaths. He used that phrase. 'Good deaths.'"

Lucy never used Delia's name, Andrew thought, just "she" and "her," as if there could not possibly be any other "she" in the world. She talked like a person who lives alone, who suddenly has the opportunity to let out the collected thoughts of a whole day.

"And so here we are," she concluded, tears shining in her black eyes, "with a big-time illness. She likes it when someone sits in the room with her, although sometimes she seems to turn off, kind of. But don't worry about that. And you don't have to be with her every minute. She likes listening to music, you might want to look through the tapes and play something. She might want something to drink—she doesn't eat any more—but she'll ask you. Whatever she wants will be in the fridge."

"Well," she said, straightening up, "I've gotta go. This meeting will start on time. I won't be late—nine, nine-thirty at the latest. Thanks so much for coming. I've gotten so I don't ever want her out of my sight, but I know that's not a good thing."

"It embarrasses me a little," Andrew said, "the way you thank me, Lucy. I'm her father, after all."

Lucy looked at him with a faint smile. She liked him a lot, enjoyed his humor and his liveliness, his little flirtations. There was something helpless about him, though, and it was annoying. It drove Delia crazy sometimes. She hoped he'd be all right, hoped they'd both be all right.

"Oh—I almost forgot. She might have to pee and she can't get up any more. Imagine," she added more to herself than to him. "Just three days ago she could manage with her walker. Anyway the bedpan is in the tub. If she has to pee she'll lift herself up and you can slip it under her and hand her a piece of toilet paper. Just empty it in the toilet when you're done and rinse it out. God! I'm so glad I didn't forget this."

Lucy grabbed her briefcase and a light jacket. She kissed Andrew on the cheek, saying, "I gotta go now, really," and whisked herself out the door.

Andrew walked down to the back of the apartment, to the master bedroom. There was Delia, nestled in her pillows, her beautiful head, her long face and high cheekbones. Her knees were up, the light quilt in folds all around her. Her hand flew up, her fingers waved lightly, "Hi Papa," she said, hoarsely.

He tried to remember when it was that she had started to call him "Papa." She'd explained that she thought she was too old for "Daddy," said something about not wanting to be one of those grown women who call their fathers "Daddy" all their lives. But she didn't like "Dad" either. Everyone, she'd said, called their fathers "Dad" as if Dad were all one person. It was too "generic," he thought she'd said. She came up with "Papa," and it had stuck.

She was wide awake.

"Hi Delia." He crossed the room and kissed her on her pale cheek, bringing to her bedside one of the many uncomfortable wooden chairs from Vermont that filled the apartment. "How're you feeling?"

"Pretty good, but I do drift off to sleep, have weird dreams. Some very nice and some awful, but I don't remember them. Except the one about the glasses of milk. I keep having that one."

He sat down. She seemed to want to talk despite the obvious effort it took. He thought he should talk to her the way Cassy did, an easy flow of words— what did they talk about?—but his mind was blank. All he could think about was that he was sitting here with his daughter who was dying.

"Glasses of milk?" he asked, making conversation.

"It's about Bernie, you know, Bernie the nurse in Dr. Castle's office. In the good dreams she brings me a big, huge glass of milk. I can see it right here in the air in front of me, and I drink it and it feels so good. I feel so good."

Andrew shifted in his chair.

"I like that dream. But other times Bernie brings

me a glass of milk and she has a smile that looks evil and I drink the glass of milk and it tastes like poison, it is poison and Bernie laughs and laughs."

"Hmmm," Andrew murmured. Then, "Do you remember when I used to give you your medicine that you hated so much when you had tonsillitis?"

"I remember."

"You were very good about it, you know."

Delia's eyes closed. He looked at her face in repose, resting against the pillow. The unwelcome thought returned: that he had missed something, that there was something to know or give that he had ignored or neglected, some moment long ago that had passed forever.

"You had a way of bearing things," Andrew said. "Do you remember when I had to sit you and Cassy down and tell you about the divorce? Do you remember what you said?"

"Tell me."

"Well, Cassy burst into tears immediately and pleaded with us not to do it and worried about what she would say to her friends. So it took me a few minutes to realize that you hadn't said anything. So I asked you, 'What do you think, Delia?'"

"You said, 'I think that if you and Mummy can't

stop yelling at each other, it will be better.' I remember thinking that you were trying to be too...too rational, so I said, 'That's true about the fighting, but it's sad, too, isn't it?' And you said, 'You're not home that much anyway, so it won't even be that different.' I was shocked. You were so clear and composed for a girl of eleven; and it was true, I guess, but you were only eleven. I was worried, and I felt accused."

"It wasn't about you, Papa. It was about me."

"Yes," he sighed. "I loved you very much, you know," he whispered more to himself than to her. He felt such a surge of grief—not about now, not about her dying, but about then, about that lost time—that it took all his strength to hold himself together.

"I'm sorry," he whispered, or maybe just thought, into Delia's silence.

Too late now, he thought, for the second time that day.

Delia, her eyes still closed, lifted her hand up, palm toward him. "Don't be sorry," she said. "I loved you, too."

Andrew thought she must be asleep. Her hair was coming in after the chemotherapy, about an inch all over her shapely head, the gray that no one, not even she, had seen in all these years of applying henna.

She reminded him of Joan of Arc, her hair like a mail hood. She looked pale, wasted, but also serene.

He tiptoed over to the tape player. Lucy said she would like some music. He picked out from a pile of tapes Schubert's *Trout Quintet*, which he pushed into the tape slot, but it wouldn't go all the way in. He pulled it out and pushed it in again, several times, but it just jammed.

"Damn!" he whispered.

He took it out and stared at it for a moment, then reversed it and put the tape part in first. This seemed to work, and he pushed "play."

"Hmmm. Nice," she said as the opening chords filled the room.

Delia stirred among her pillows, her eyes fluttering for a moment, opening then closing. He peered at her face. She looked uncomfortable, frowning, muttering to herself. Her eyes opened.

"Bedpan." Her face seemed to harden a little and she looked away.

Andrew went into the adjoining bathroom, flipped the light switch. The bedpan was just where Lucy said it would be, white enamel, heavier than he had imagined. He stared at it a moment, wondering which way it went, then decided it was obvious—narrow end toward the back. He rehearsed what Lucy had told him: Delia would lift her body and he would slip it under.

He came back to the bed. Delia's eyes were closed. She seemed asleep.

"I have the bedpan," Andrew leaned toward her.

Without opening her eyes, without acknowledging him, she raised her pelvis up.

Andrew hesitated, then lifted the bedcovers and slipped the bedpan under her, pushing her nightshirt out of the way; he stood by waiting for a cue. There was a silence.

"I need a tissue." Her eyes were still shut.

Lucy had said toilet paper. He went back into the bathroom and unrolled some toilet paper, regarded it, then rolled out some more, thinking it was not enough. Better to have too much he thought, closing his hands over the huge mound. He put it in her hand, lying open on the quilt.

"Can't. I'm too tired."

Andrew took the wad of paper and stood for a moment, not knowing what to do.

"Shall I?"

There was no answer. Her eyes were closed, and

he couldn't read her expression.

He lifted the bedclothes again, just enough to feel his way over her thigh, move down and dab her crotch where he thought he should, then brought his hand with the wad out. He went back to the bathroom, holding the wad of paper away from his body, threw it into the toilet, then went back to stand by the bed again.

"I'm taking the bedpan now."

Again she pushed her pelvis up. Andrew pulled the bedpan out and walked carefully into the bathroom. Her urine was a shocking dark red.

The Schubert had stopped playing, perhaps had been finished for some time. Delia was still asleep or not present. Her face looked peaceful again. I've not been such a bad father, have I? Andrew wanted to say, had wanted to say all evening.

Her eyes opened. Her hand went up, her fingers fluttered: "Hi, Papa."

Andrew smiled, still standing where he could really see her in the high, old-fashioned bed.

"I'm dying," she said, seeming to wake up. "Dr. Castle helped me figure that out. I kept saying something was wrong with my stomach—so bloated, so gassy. If we could only get it down I would be all right. And then Cassy said maybe it wasn't really my stomach, that maybe I should ask Dr. Castle why I was so bloated. I did and he said it was not really my stomach, it was my liver. That's all he said. That's how I realized that I was dying."

"I'll miss you," Andrew said. "You're brave, you've always been brave," he said.

Delia frowned. "Please don't say that, Papa. I'm just me. There's nothing brave here. Just be here with me."

"In ways that I am usually not?" he found himself saying, wishing immediately he hadn't.

Delia was silent for a moment

"You give what you love, Papa, not necessarily what people need. But what you love is its own gift."

Her eyes closed and they sat for a long time in silence. Andrew thought about what she had just said, wondering if he understood it, whether it was what he was hoping for. When she looked at him again he asked, "Would you like the Schubert again, or something else?"

"The Schubert. But you know what I really, really want?"

She was wide awake now. She held him with her

eyes, her hand stretched out on the quilt toward him.

He took her hand, "What?"

"A big drink of papaya juice from Papaya King, that's what I want."

"Sure," he said. "It's in the fridge?"

"No. I haven't thought of it 'til now. You'd have to go get it."

What about leaving her alone?

"It's all right to leave me," she said. "I'm not going anywhere; nothing's going to happen to me yet."

Andrew felt anxious and considered calling Elly.

"Well, I suppose that's true. And it's still open?"

"Papaya King is open until midnight. Every night. It's down on Seventy-Second and Broadway."

"I know where it is. You sure you'll be all right?"

'I'm sure. All I want is a big drink of papaya juice, nice and cold the way they make it there. I haven't had any in years."

"Papaya juice? Nothing else?"

"Nothing else."

"Okay," he said. "One papaya juice coming up for my lovely daughter." He kissed Delia on the cheek and left the room.

Andrew hailed a cab on Broadway. He had seen Papaya King a thousand times, its brightly lit front, its garish orange and green sign, its cartoon character in the shape of a papaya. It was famous. Best hot dogs in the neighborhood.

The cab dodged through traffic, made a U-turn, and pulled up.

"Please wait," Andrew asked the cabby as he hoisted himself out of the taxi.

He was third in line at the counter. As he waited, he jiggled the change in his pocket. When his turn came, he asked the red-faced boy in the Papaya King cap for a large papaya juice to go. In a matter of moments he had the big, waxy cup in his hand, had capped it and grabbed a straw, paid, and then, at the last minute, laying out an extra dollar and change, said, "I'll take a hot dog, too." This he slathered with relish and mustard, then rushed back to the waiting cab.

He held the papaya juice between his knees and stuffed the hot dog into his mouth. The sharp, intense mustard and sweet relish, mixing with the spiciness of the meat, burst in his mouth and he realized how hungry he'd been. The cab sped up Broadway, made the turn onto West End, and pulled up to Delia's building. Andrew looked at his watch. He hadn't been gone for more than twenty minutes.

Back in the apartment, Delia lay on her pillows, knees up, just as he had left her. She was alert, and she lifted her thin hand from the quilt.

"Thanks Papa."

Andrew retrieved the straw he had stuffed into his jacket, tore the paper off, and after several unsuccessful stabs, pushed it through the hole in the cover. He handed it to Delia and hovered, thinking she might need help, but she grasped the cup and sucked vigorously on the straw, taking three long draughts.

"Mmmm…heaven," she said, smiling and closing her eyes.

When it slipped from Delia's hand, Andrew retrieved the cup, put it aside, and gently squeezed her shoulder. He sat himself down on his chair by the bed to await Lucy's return and his walk home alone in the dark.

Hardball

Softball is for sissies. Everyone in the fourth grade agrees. First of all, the ball is light for its size, clumsy and too big for small hands. Second, softball is not what real baseball players play. Only kids and girls play softball. That's what all the kids think, but that's what they get to play in school anyway. Hardball, the teachers all say, is too dangerous. So they play hardball after school in Riverside Park down by the Hudson River.

On this Monday afternoon the "hardball kids," as they think of themselves, get together as usual for a game. And as usual, there are only six kids, so they divide into threes, pitcher, first baseman (foot on David's backpack), fielder in the field, and three batters at the plate, which is Tommy's jacket. The batters take turns acting as catcher.

Laura is first up and after swinging at David's wild pitch, she hits the second pitch out into the field and makes the run to first easily.

Tommy, up next, gets a hit but, heading for first, runs smack into Laura, who is on her way home. They both tumble to the ground. David races out and touches each of them with the ball.

"You're out," he shrieks with a big grin on his face. "Two outs!"

"No fair!" Tommy yells.

"It is fair. You're both out."

The start of an argument, and no telling where it would go: just yelling, or pummeling, too? It's enough to move all of them out of their places: Ivan waiting to bat, David on the "mound," Sophie in the field, Greg on first base, Laura and Tommy, all of them leave the safety and order of their places and move towards each other, their hearts pounding with excitement and dread.

"They bumped into each other. It was an accident. We should call a time-out. It's not fair to put them out," (Ivan.)

"They should watch where they're going, that's what. They're out." (David.)

"They are not."

"Out, out, out," David shoves his face close to Ivan's.

"Not out—not!" Ivan looks flustered and his big glasses move down his nose.

"Ivan's right, and stop pushing at him," Laura shrieks, moving toward David, whose fair skin is suffused with red under his yellow thatch of hair.

"You know, Ivan's got a point," Sophie, who's been standing on the edge of the group, says. "It was an accident. Accidents aren't a part of the game. We should have a rule for accidents."

"How can you make a rule about accidents?" Greg asks. "I think they're out."

They've been standing in two little knots, arms akimbo, taking sides. As one, they all turn a little toward Sophie.

"But anything could be an accident, you could trip—then what?" David looks around for agreement.

Greg mutters, "Yeah, anything could be an accident."

"Well, but we're always banging into each other running bases—that's an accident. And if we had a rule—"

"What kind of rule? There isn't any rule about that in real baseball."

"But they have three bases so they don't run into each other," Ivan yells as if David were hard of hearing.

"I know!" That's Greg. "Like if the two runners smack into each other we have a time-out."

"What good would that do, stupid?" David again. "They're out, that should be the rule. They smack into each other, they should watch where they're going, they're out. We don't even have to tap them. They're just out." He crosses his arms.

Silence.

Then, "No, no." Sophie holds up her hand. "Not they're out. How about they smack into each other and we have a do-over?"

"A do-over? What do you do over?"

"You send the runner to first back home and the other guy back to first and you pitch again. You start from before the accident. A do-over."

Silence. David's fists are at his sides, his knuckles white.

Ivan says, "Then we wouldn't have to interrupt the game and have big fights about what to do." He blinks.

More silence.

"We could make a rule about accidents that says we have a do-over when there's an accident," says Greg.

Then, without another word, the children straggle back across the grass to their places and Tommy gets up to bat again.

They play for another hour, until the sun begins to go down. It's time to go home. They walk in small groups down Riverside Drive, gradually going in different directions. Tommy and Ivan, who live in the same apartment house, turn into Eighty-Ninth[th] Street.

"David is a big bully," Ivan says.

"Yeah," says Tommy.

"Do-overs is a great idea, don't you think?"

"Yeah."

The sun is slipping behind the skyscrapers across the river in New Jersey, casting long shadows on the sidewalk in front of them. The street is busy with people returning home from work. Ivan pulls hard at the big glass and wrought iron door at number 320. He and Tommy stand by the elevator waiting for Bob to bring it back to the lobby.

Mrs. Digby's Picture Album

In clearing out the many mysterious objects of her father's estate, the auctioneer's only heir impulsively set aside a photo album containing pictures of no one she knew, with a sheaf of unsigned papers tucked into it, of which the following is a facsimile. It matters not for whom this was intended, nor to what end—it is your story now.

Album found in the torn-down wall of an old house "Narrator" (first person or third?) is in the process of renovating. Modest country house to retire to from New York City to get away from it all, and do what she has always wanted to do: go through years of unfinished essays and journals and write a memoir or a collection of personal essays, the story of her life and times, something to leave behind. Coming across the album, something forgotten, personal, left behind, is a welcome distraction. Promises to be fascinating. She is, deep inside, a snoop, a spy, an outsider. She can't wait to pore over its pages.

I settle in a chair in the living room (*note:* first person works better) with the album in my lap. On the cover, neatly printed, "Mrs. Digby's Photo Album." There are no dates, but there are clues that tell me the album was made over a period of time most likely beginning somewhere in the mid-thirties. On the first page, a large, borderless print of a woman, boyish-looking with narrow hips and long legs, smiling out at the photographer, her arm encircling a baby on her hip. There's something flapperish about her short hair and the silky fabric of her simple shirt—a "shift," I think it would have been called—falling loosely over her hips. Her broad smile reveals perfect teeth. The baby stares out at the photographer with serious eyes.

Slightly behind them stands a man, slim, with dark curly hair and a hawklike nose. His eyes are cast downward almost as if he is looking at, or into, himself. I feel that I don't like him. I can't say why.

They pose in a room, a parlor, next to a velvet love seat behind which hangs a large painting, a dramatic landscape—of the Hudson River School, I think. Sun coming in from a side window casting a line across the Oriental rug and lighting up the baby's fair, curly hair. The photo is beautifully composed, an iconic family portrait. The elegant setting, though, cannot be the house I just bought. How, I wonder, did it come to be in the walls of this house?

A few pages later—a murky photo, underexposed. A woman, perhaps in her late forties, robust, attractive, wearing a cotton housedress, leaning with a rag over a closed piano. I follow her gaze to the floor where the baby girl sits, her arms stretched out toward the woman. This must be the Digbys' nanny or the housekeeper. Mother, father, baby (a girl, I am certain), and housekeeper. Parlor with a velvet sofa. I am hooked.

As I move page by page through the album, the baby grows into childhood and early adolescence, the mother and father grow imperceptibly older, he putting on weight, she more insistently smiling, both with something, a shadow, across their faces that was not there before. They, all three, swim in lakes; ride waves in the ocean; picnic on a grassy knoll; play croquet on the front lawn; throw snowballs; ski downhill; host backyard parties (father standing at the barbecue) and elegant dinner parties inside at a long candlelit table. The photographs, all in black and white, are not your usual family snapshots: they are, with only a few exceptions, balanced, in composition and in the play of light and shadow. Sharp and clear or soft and slightly blurred by turns, depending on the subject. They are exquisite. Who takes them? A friend who is a photographer, perhaps. Someone gifted, certainly.

The baby grows into a little girl, then a bigger one, then almost a young lady. By the time she is seven, eight, her hair is dark like her father's. The photographer catches her unawares most of the time, catches a serious girl focused intently on whatever she is doing: banging her spoon on the kitchen table, dressing a baby doll, weaving potholders on a little metal frame, reading in the crook of a tree. I shuffle back through pages and forward again to my stopping place. The photographer loves this child. I can see it.

There are two pages of delightful pictures of smiling girls in party clothes, ribbons in their hair, stiff taffeta dresses—another time—posing, smiling under a large maple, playing pin-the-tail-on-the-donkey, eating cake at the picnic table. In one, the girl stands with her father, about to mount a pogo stick. A birthday present?

Every so often there is a photo of the housekeeper (housekeeper/nanny—can't figure her out) tying the girl's shoes, braiding her hair, handing her up to the school bus in the early morning light, kissing her on the tip of her head. The child's smiles are reserved for this caretaker. These are just snapshots, a little off kilter, amateurish. Not like the others, but charming nevertheless. Taken perhaps by the mother? The father?

The family travels to faraway places. Florence I recognize immediately and neighboring stone towns, narrow streets, open piazzas. The countryside of Ireland, I think, then Paris. Beautiful shots of the succession of bridges across the Seine, of the girl, older now, poring over books at open bookstalls, of the rose window at Sainte Chapelle. Taken together, the pictures catch the peculiar beauty of this City of Light.

The housekeeper, her plain but handsome face peering out from under a mannish hat with a brim, goes everywhere with them. Shows up in snapshots with the girl always at her side.

Then, closer to home, the rocky coast of Nova Scotia I'm sure, and the Smokies I'm pretty sure, San Francisco, Yellowstone Park—all in black and white, which brings to the scenes a strong sense of light and shadow as form. I never miss colors, not even of the rose window in Paris.

On a later page a photo of the girl and the housekeeper, almost the same height now, hugging by a car, beside which stands an old-fashioned trunk, a school trunk, the father waiting by the open passenger door. Must be the mother who took the picture. The baby girl now almost a young woman. Serious, with the dark eyes and curly black hair of her father. I like her. She must be going away to school, I think. The housekeeper is sad, I think.

A bit past here the father disappears. I don't realize it right away, but at some point I begin to leaf backwards a few pages in the book, thinking I haven't seen him, must have missed him. The photo of the girl going away is the last picture of him. I miss him. I had come to like him better as I got to know them, his quiet reflectiveness. And to like the mother less, annoyed by her histrionic smile.

Has he died? I peer, now, into their faces—mother's, daughter's, friends in the backyard—looking for signs of grief, or sadness, or tiredness, but I find none. The mother's smile never fails, and the child has her usual look of concentration on what she is doing, rewarding only the photographer with a direct gaze and an occasional, quiet smile. Still the same photographer. Still the same qualities, photographs that vividly chronicle a way of life, character, and love.

In the few pages left, photos are tucked haphazardly, not mounted. Miscellaneous photos of the girl, her friends. One of the mother, with longer hair now, swept up in the back with a pile of curls on the top of her head, her skirts long, down to her ankles. The "new look" I think, late forties, wartime. And always—her smile—a smile for some unseen audience—the photographer? Or is it just that she is always "on stage"—the smile that lights her face, reveals her perfect teeth.

And so the album tells of a family, a growing child, a life of privilege and richness, of good fortune, and of rupture. Only the pictures speak, the captions tell nothing, not even the names of the girl, her mother and father. A family of three, the Digbys as I've thought of them, sometimes appear, with the child on one hip or the other, the girl, curly-haired like her father, standing between both parents, growing taller, gaining on them, but more often just father and child or mother and child, occasionally housekeeper and child. And, in the full-page shots, just the child. Blowing out candles at her birthday, riding horseback in a field, standing among a group of children in her Halloween costume (a witch), snuggling comfortably in the crook of a tree limb, high off the ground, reading a book, breasts showing through her cotton shirts, wearing lipstick, leaving home.

But then something happens.

Have the parents separated, divorced, the mother and the father, she an outward, smiling person bent on charming everyone, he always looking inward, his mind on something inside? He hasn't died, I've decided.

Who is this photographer? A friend of the father, the mother? Someone who's around all the time, a constant and welcome presence it would seem. Someone who's still there after they divorce, at least for a while. A relative perhaps? Whoever it is, the photographer loves the child.

And the album—who put it together, arranged it so lovingly over the years? The photographer, unbeknownst to the family? Who then presented it years later? Or never delivered it? Or maybe, more likely, the mother, who saved the pictures over the years and then made the album? Somehow, I don't think so.

What about the amateurish pictures included in this beautiful album? Of the child and the nanny. These pictures are taken by the mother? The father? And included in the album?

Who lived in my house and saved the album?

The girl? What happened to the girl?

Not wanting to miss anything, I leaf through the remaining empty pages to the last page. "Mrs. Digby's Picture Album," it announces here, again, as at the beginning. Underneath the title, centered and penned in the same white ink as in the captions:

The Whitman Family
Pictures by Mrs. Digby
1932–1952

I close the album.

Mrs. Digby!

I close my eyes, flooded with my sense of Mrs. Digby. This work of art she has left behind, about a family, about herself.

I hold the album on my lap, hug it. I am envying Mrs. Digby, her embrace of life (the life she found? chose?), a woman loved and loving, I think, not afraid to love, the child, the girl. A story all bound up in the pages of this old, forgotten album.

Where did she go when the girl grew up? When the rupture happened? What about Mr. Digby?

I can't help thinking about myself. Alone, in my late sixties. Obsessed with this meticulous renovation of an old farmhouse in this lovely rural valley. Leaving everything behind. Human entanglements that have always disconcerted me, kept me at a distance, estranged—from my daughter, who sided with her father, my ex-husband; my lover of twenty years, who stayed with his wife.

I get up from my chair and go to my study. Sit at my desk, open my computer, and scroll through to the beginning of my memoir. Not engaging. Not so far. Not right now. Close it down and create a new document. I take a deep breath.

At the top I write "Mrs. Digby's Picture Album." I will write about life and loving and leaving and letting go.

Playmates

Sasha bursts through the break in the hemlock hedge between her house and the Bennetts' next door. Clad in jeans and a bright pink t-shirt, she carries a shoebox under her arm, which she shifts from one arm to the other as she runs up the front steps and knocks on the door.

Edith's mother peers through the darkness of the screen door.

"Can Edith come out to play?"

"Just a moment, Sasha, I'll go tell her you're here."

Sasha has spent the morning alone. She has spent a lot of time alone this summer. Her parents are living apart. Her mother goes off every afternoon to work at the bookstore in town. Her sister is at a music and dance camp. Her own summer-school art classes, where she made linoleum prints, are over and now she has three long weeks before fifth grade begins. She will take the train and visit her father in New York for a weekend, but mostly there's nothing to do and some days she'll just be by herself. Her mother has a boyfriend and sometimes goes out with him. This makes Sasha nervous because she's terrified of the dark.

Mrs. Bennett disappears into the house and soon

after, Edith pushes through the door and stands on the top step, smiling her odd, crooked smile, smoothing her faded cotton dress. Edith always wears dresses, even after school and on weekends. Her face is smooth and round. She's not ugly, but different. She looks old, ancient, like the old Eskimo women they studied in school, with squinty eyes and a faraway expression, as if she's looking at something no one else can see. They're in the same class, but Sasha avoids Edith in school. It's almost as if they don't know each other and anyway, Edith isn't like other kids and is always on her own. Sasha plays with her on weekends when there isn't anybody else.

Edith is always happy to come out and play. Sasha tries to teach her things she should know. She tells Edith that she should grow her hair out and wear it in a ponytail. "Like me," she says. But Edith pays no attention. Sasha tries to get her to wear jeans on weekends. Edith always smiles and says she will, but then doesn't. Ditto saddle shoes. Now, Edith looks down at her big brown shoes, waiting, it seems, for Sasha to announce what they are going to do.

"C'mon down, Edith, I have something to show you. Then we can go over to my house or to the brook."

Mrs. Bennett pokes her head out the door.

"Not too far, girls," she says before disappearing again.

Edith makes her way down the steps, her pudgy body swaying from side to side. She sits down on the bottom step next to Sasha.

"I brought my trading cards," Sasha announces, balancing the shoebox on her knees. She has spent the morning organizing them. "See? I have them in sets here and singles here." She flips through two sections of trading cards separated by Popsicle sticks. All the girls except Edith have trading cards. Sasha pulls four cards from the box.

"This is a complete set. It's worth much more than a broken set." She holds up and fans a blue, red, yellow, and green version of Gainsborough's *Little Boy Blue*. "I just traded Sandy one Springer Spaniel with a red background for the blue and green Boy Blues. Sandy really wanted the dog because she has two more, in green and blue." Sasha puts the cards down on the step and rummages in her box.

"Sandy has more cards than anyone. That's because her father buys a whole pack with a picture she wants and she takes one for her collection and throws the rest away. You're supposed to get your cards by trading and you just have to wait until a good trade comes along. You don't buy cards. That's not fair, but Sandy's mother is in a mental hospital, so we don't say anything."

Sasha takes cards out and files them in the back.

"Sandy and Jenny are playing at Jenny's house today," she says. Earlier, she had called Sandy to invite her over to play. Sandy lives a mile down the road with her father. They are very rich and live in a big house with dark, shiny leather furniture. Her father has a deep voice and a black mustache; he always has a tan and in his hand, a drink tinkling with ice. Sandy had said she couldn't come, she was going over to Jenny's. Jenny is Sasha's friend, too, so how come they hadn't invited her?

Sasha picks up the Little Boy Blues again and fans them out for Edith to see.

"This is my favorite set. I wouldn't trade these for anything. The way this works, Edith, is you collect cards from anyone, your parents or friends, just to get started, and then you trade with other girls and you try to get sets. You might give two singles for one that would give you a set. Or you might give away a really good card for three to get your collection bigger. See?" Sasha takes out several cards and fans them out.

Edith leans over and peers at the cards. She

reaches out and takes one at a time, turns it over. She looks for a long time at the jack of spades or the three of diamonds on the other side and hands it back. Suddenly, she points at one—of a leaping dog—and smiles.

"You can have that card if you want it," Sasha says. "I'm pretty sure it doesn't come in a set."

Edith takes the card.

"I like the dog," she says. "Thank you, Sasha."

"If you want to start a collection and trade with everyone, I could give you some more," Sasha says.

"That's okay," Edith says. "I like the dog."

Sasha replaces the cards in the box behind the last Popsicle stick and sets the box down on the steps with a thump. She leans forward, elbows on knees, chin in hands, and stares out at the lawn. She doesn't know what to do next. Once in a while, a car whooshes by.

"I tell you what," she says suddenly, jumping up. "Let's go down by the brook and throw stones."

Edith stays where she is and seems to shrink back a little.

"C'mon, Edith. We'll have fun. I'll leave my cards here on the steps."

Edith gets up, her face brightening.

"Okay," She turns back into the house, card in hand. "I'm just putting the dog away."

A few minutes later, rocking sideways, she lumbers back down the steps and follows Sasha across the lawn out onto Nod Hill Road. The black tar shimmers in the heat. The sound of cicadas fills the air. Sweat runs down Edith's face, and Sasha flaps the bottom of her t-shirt in and out to send cooling air up to her chest. Except for the buzzing insects, the day is quiet. Nothing moves. No cars pass. The children are alone.

When they reach the part of the road that is a bridge, Sasha shimmies down the embankment beneath the road to the brook and watches as Edith hesitates, then turns and crawls down backwards. Sasha thinks how foolish she looks.

"You look like a baby, Edith," she calls out, laughing. But she is mad. Why can't Edith do anything?

Edith gets to the bottom and laughs a little. She smoothes the front of her dress with her hands.

The brook runs noisily over a ground of pebbles; the moss on big rocks waves like green hair in the running water. This is one of Sasha's favorite places to come when she's alone. The water in the middle of the stream is deeper, a golden brown. She loves crossing the stream from rock to rock. Sometimes, she falls in and goes home with wet jeans and shoes, wet all over, which annoys her mother.

"Let's play soldier and baby, Edith. I'll be an American soldier in France hiding from the Nazis and you'll be the baby. We can be hiding over there, under the bridge."

"I don't want to get my shoes wet." Edith looks alarmed.

"Well, we can go along the bank here and then, see, there's sand on the edge of the brook under the bridge. We can pretend we're in danger from the Nazis, and we're hiding under the bridge. We can hear them marching above us, and it's very loud and scary. You're a French baby I found in a field crying and I'm protecting you."

"No," Edith says, "I don't want to."

Sasha gives up. She knows Edith can be stubborn and that when she says "no" she doesn't change.

Sasha stands for a moment listening to the sound of the water and the jangle of stones in the bottom rolling against each other. She picks up a stone and throws it into the middle of the brook.

"Well, then let's have a stone-throwing contest and see who can get it over to the other side of the brook, okay?" Edith nods.

"You can go first."

Edith smiles her squinty smile and bends over to pick up a stone. She straightens, looks at Sasha, then swings her arm straight up over her head, lets go, and the stone falls at her feet.

"You didn't really throw it. Watch me."

Sasha picks up the stone and throws it with all her might, aiming across the brook. It falls short, plunking into the water.

"Everyone gets two chances a turn," she says, and she winds her arm up again, lets go of the stone, and it sails across the stream and into the grasses on the other side.

"Now you try it."

"Okay." Edith bends down for a stone and holds her arm up over her head again, thrusts it forward. The stone falls a little farther from her feet this time.

"I can't do it like you."

"No, not straight over your head like that. Here, this way." And Sasha shows her, just like their gym teacher did, demonstrating how to throw softballs; how to tilt her body, draw her arm back sideways with her arm still bent, and throw with all her might, just like a boy. The second stone also lands on the other side of the brook.

"I can't," says Edith.

"You can. Just do it like this. Watch this."

"I don't want to," Edith says.

"Oh Edith, we can't have a contest if you don't try," Why couldn't she throw a stone like everyone else?

"Okay." Edith picks up a stone but lets it slide out of her hand onto the ground.

"I don't like this game."

"Oh, Edith. You're no fun." Why couldn't she just play? Why can't she do anything? Sasha gives her a shove, and giggles a little as if she was making a joke. Edith stumbles and falls into the water.

Sasha's scared and thinks of running away and leaving Edith there, on her back, struggling to get out of the water. She can't get herself over and up. Sasha wades in and grabs Edith's hand, but Edith pulls so hard and feels so heavy that Sasha loses her grip and goes down, too, into the water. She gets up on her hands and knees, stands up, and gets hold of Edith's arm again, her whole arm with both her hands. Edith is still on her back and can't get up.

"I'm trying to pull you up."

Edith looks frightened.

Sasha says, "It's shallow, you won't drown or anything. I promise." She keeps pulling. She wants everything to stop happening. She wants to take it all back. She didn't mean for this to happen. Finally, Edith grabs onto a boulder with her free hand. Sasha keeps pulling and Edith manages to get up onto her feet.

"You pushed me down," she says, shivering in her wet dress, dragging her feet out of the water. "Why did you push me down?"

"It was just a joke. You know, like kids pushing each other around in school. I didn't mean to hurt you, Edith, I didn't mean to. I'm sorry I pushed you. I didn't know you would fall down." By now Sasha was almost crying.

The girls stand on the bank, silent. They're both wet, their clothes sticking to their bodies. Sasha pulls Edith's dress down in the back and pulls her own t-shirt away from her body. Edith pushes hair away from her face. Her barrette has slipped down by her ear.

"You better take your barrette out or it'll fall off," Sasha says.

Edith removes it and clutches it in her hand. Without talking, they turn toward the bank. Sasha climbs up, throwing her arm out every so often to keep her balance. Edith crawls up on all fours. When she gets to the top, they start slowly up the road together.

"Your mother's going to be mad," Sasha breaks their silence.

"You pushed me."

They stop for a moment and Sasha looks directly at Edith. "But I didn't mean to. It was an accident, just an accident. I didn't know you would fall in." She is desperate to erase what she has done, to believe she didn't mean it.

They move on.

"If you tell your mother I pushed you, she won't let you play with me any more."

"I like to play with you, Sasha."

"Me, too. I liked showing you my trading cards. I like to play with you."

"Then we fell in." Edith smiled.

"We did," Sasha says, "We both fell in and got wet."

Days go by. Sasha waits for Mrs. Bennett to call her mother. She worries that she will be found out and punished. Her mother will be very angry. Everybody in school will hear about it—the new teacher, the principal. But days go by and nobody says anything. Sasha goes to New York to visit her father and forgets all about it until school starts up again. On the first day, there's Edith in the hall, coming toward her, smiling her lopsided smile. Sasha says "Hi," looks down, and keeps moving.

177

Ashes, Ashes

"I feel them sitting in my closet," Jonathan said. "Unfinished business. I need to bring it to closure—I think that's the word 'grief people' use. I want to do something just right, but I can't seem to come up with anything."

My half-brother was calling me about the ashes that had been sitting in his closet from 2004 and 2005, respectively. Here it was, five years later. I understood the dilemma. What would be the right thing to do with the remains of our father and his third wife Barbara, who was Jonathan's mother.

"Lately, I've been wondering whether we could maybe bury them in your backyard, whether you or Caroline would mind?"

"Mind? No, not at all. We could certainly bury them here."

"I think it's…kind of…only if we can't come up with anything else," he said.

"More a solution than an inspiration?"

"Exactly."

Even as we spoke, I didn't really want them in our backyard. What would we do with them? Would we mark them with some kind of monument? A gravestone? Or just bury them and walk by? Stop and have a moment of silence from time to time? And then, the time would come when we'd leave, or die, and there they'd be, anonymous, forgotten. Uninvited, these thoughts ran through my head. Did I not care? I hadn't been thinking about their ashes. I had said goodbye to my father at his memorial service and to Barbara at hers.

"I've thought of the Sound off Montauk Point," he continued, "where we vacationed when I was a little boy. I don't think you were ever out there with us, were you?"

That sounded like a really nice idea, like the kind of thing people did with ashes, scattering them over water on a beautiful day. But the childhood memory of my father at the beach interfered with this pleasant prospect. He didn't take off his shoes and socks; he'd stand in his pants and a short-sleeved button-down shirt staring out at swimmers—almost as if they were aliens. Then he might sit for a short while in a beach chair under an umbrella, struggle with his newspaper to keep it open in the breeze, and brush sand off his pant legs, the paper, wherever it collected—a losing battle. Finally he'd give up and say something apologetic about its being too hot, wave and smile and troop back to the car, where he'd sit in the driver's seat with the door open, peacefully engrossed in the news of the day. The fact was, Dad and Barbara were not beach people. They were hopelessly urban.

"Unless he totally changed by the time you came along," I said, "he wasn't really much of a water person. Not a nature person at all. Remember how he always retracted his hand if a cat came near him, or a dog? We had a cat when I was little and he wasn't nasty or unpleasant to the cat, he just didn't want it anywhere near him."

Jonathan laughed. "You're right. The Long Island Sound doesn't exactly call either of them to mind."

When Jonathan was born I was twenty-six and lived nearby, in the same neighborhood, on New York's Upper West Side. Barbara was my father's third wife, Jonathan his third child. Tom, his son from his second marriage to Myrna, was an artist living in Seattle. At twenty-six, I was busy with my own life and didn't spend much time with this third family.

I remembered when Dad made the shocking announcement that he and Barbara were moving to Tucson for Barbara's health.

"Tucson!" Jonathan called me, upset.

We couldn't believe it. We believed removing our father at eighty-two from New York would hasten his decline, would probably kill him. Tucson wasn't on any map we carried around in our heads. But of course we helped them—Jonathan more than I. We sorted, threw away, went through mountains of stuff and memories—packed them up and helped them leave the city we considered their natural habitat. The whole process brought Jonathan and me closer, made us good friends.

"What about we scatter their ashes on the Hudson River off Riverside Drive Park? Down the street from where they lived until 1994," he said.

"But I guess we'd have to hire a boat," he added.

"There's always the Gardetto plot in Middleton," I said. "I don't think you've ever seen it. It's beautiful, goes all the way back to Giacomo and Maria Gardetto who came here in 1883. It's peaceful and it's Dad's roots." I found the idea appealing as we talked.

"Hmm. Trouble is, it has nothing to do with Barbara. And anyway, I always think of Middleton as the place he wanted to get away from."

"He wanted to get away, but he loved going back there for family gatherings—a funeral or his mother's birthday—whatever. He actually said to me once as we were driving up to his brother's funeral, 'I love a

Middleton funeral.' Can you believe it?"

But it had nothing to do with Barbara. The more we considered it the more complicated it seemed. Jonathan had not even met our grandmother. Dad had kept his second divorce and third marriage a secret from his mother. He always said it was his sister's idea. Their mother was aging and fragile and it would kill her to learn that he'd gotten divorced again, his sister had told him. And so from the time he and Barbara were married until his mother died, Dad always said during the annual Christmas phone call that Tom was out playing or at a friend's house, and Myrna was in the shower and sent her love.

"Other families," Jonathan said toward the end of our conversation, "other families probably don't have ashes lying around for years. I mean they know what to do when someone dies, don't you think?"

"Who knows about other families," I said, perhaps unhelpfully. Our father's life of disconnected chapters, of reinvention, made it hard to figure out how to do just the right thing with his and Barbara's ashes.

That evening at dinner, I asked Caroline what was done after her parents' deaths.

"They were cremated, my father five years before my mother. And their ashes were buried where my mother wanted them. It was pretty straightforward."

"So they're there and you're here."

"Yes. They're where my mother wanted them to be, but not any place I'm ever likely to be again. There's no way to avoid that. Did you ever ask your father what he wanted? Did Jonathan ask Barbara?"

"I don't know about Jonathan, but I asked Dad once. Maybe it was my imagination, but I was sure his face lit up when I mentioned the family plot in Middleton. And in that same conversation, not long before he died, I asked him if he wanted to be cremated. He looked at me with a funny smile and said, "Maybe not because...well...just to be on the safe side." I was shocked. He was an avowed atheist. I remember thinking, 'Once a Catholic, always a Catholic." I couldn't have been more surprised. What I do know is that Barbara wanted them both to be cremated."

"Sometimes I look at you," Caroline said, "and think what a blessing it is to come from a boring family."

I lay in bed that night feeling flummoxed. Everything about our parents was bound up with the Upper West

Side. It had derailed us, the fact that they spent their last years in Tucson, surprisingly happy as it turned out. If they had died in their city apartment, what would we have done?

With that question came the answer. How had we not thought of it before? We would have scattered their ashes somewhere in Riverside Park. Somewhere near the path where Barbara wheeled Jonathan in his stroller when he was little, where I, as an adolescent, wheeled Tom when he was little. Where Dad played catch on lazy Sunday afternoons, first with Tom, then, twelve years later, with Jonathan. It was their place, their roots, our roots, too. Dad would love it. Barbara would love it. It was perfect.

"I love it," Jonathan said when I suggested this, "I love it." He paused. "Probably Maggie is too young to participate and we should leave her at home?"

Maggie was four.

"Probably, but it's up to you and Angie," I said. Then I suddenly felt cautious.

"You know, it just occurred to me, scattering ashes in the park may be illegal." I tried to picture how we would do this in such a public place. "I can't imagine it's allowed."

"Well, we'll have to sort of sneak." Then, perhaps

worried that I might not, he added, "Will you do it?"

"Of course."

"I'm not sure I'm up for this," Jonathan announced as he and Angie took up their places across the table from us. As planned, we were meeting for a late lunch at Dock's, a brass and glass seafood restaurant on Eighty-Ninth Street and Broadway. It was a Sunday and quiet and there were few diners at this hour.

"I'm not sure about this. Maybe we should do the river after all," Jonathan said. "Quicker and less conspicuous," he added.

"It's not so easy to get—"

"No, I know, you're right. But I might not be able to do it."

"Did you bring the ashes?"

"Oh yes. They're right here." He patted the faded orange canvas bag hanging from his shoulder and placed it on the floor by his chair.

"Right here," he said again, grinning at me, his long, handsome face reminding me of both of them, Barbara and Dad.

"So, we'll think of it as an experiment."

"An exploration," Caroline added.

"Yes, an exploration," I said. "We'll go down

to the park and see what it feels like and if we don't like the way it feels, if it's not private enough, then, well, we won't do it. And if we do, we will." I felt myself getting into the spirit of making it up as we went along.

"And I know just the place." Jonathan leaned forward. "You know that rocky outcrop at the top of the park? The 'big rock,' my friends and I used to call it when we played there. It looks out over the river and the playground and it's right at the end of Eighty-Fifth Street. That's where I'd like their ashes to be."

"That sounds perfect," I said.

"Maybe we should buy a trowel so we can dig a hole and bury them if it feels too conspicuous," Angie suggested.

"That might make us more conspicuous. I think it's probably best just to sprinkle them," Caroline said.

"Scatter," Jonathan corrected. "I think we say 'scatter the ashes.'"

A Gardetto through and through I thought as we ordered our food, various selections of fresh, beautifully prepared seafood and crisp salads.

How we got onto the topic of how to talk to children, to Maggie in particular, about God I don't now remember, but the next thing I knew we were discussing children and religion. Jonathan said they didn't plan to bring Maggie up in any religion, so he worried about exposing her to religious thinking of any kind. They had recently brought Maggie to a service at an Episcopal church where Angie's parents belonged. Angie didn't think it would have any big influence on her.

"I think people get a sense of community from belonging to a church," she said. "It's not so easy to create one. Life feels so fractured with work and getting there and getting home and picking up the children. It's not so much the religion, it's the coming together every week, the ritual, that I'm attracted to. And it's…it's being quiet."

"I'm not against community, or 'quiet,' as Angie calls it," Jonathan said. "But spirituality is not the same thing as religion. I hope Maggie is able to feel her connection to others, to all of life. The wonder and mystery of nature. But she's a child and I don't want her to participate exactly because she is a child. I don't want her to believe something we don't. So I was not in favor of it. But we did take her and it was okay, fine, really. Although I wouldn't want to do it again very soon."

How striking it was that the subject of God had come up in this group of, as far as I knew, committed nonbelievers.

We lingered over our coffee.

"Good lunch," I said.

Silence.

"So, how shall we do this?" Angie spoke up.

"I brought the wooden box my mom had for Dad's ashes," Jonathan said.

I remembered the box, on her chest of drawers in their Tucson bedroom, made of walnut and decorated with turquoise stones. I wondered back then if I would want Caroline's ashes lying around the house, if it came to that—or mine.

"I didn't get a box for Mom's ashes," he said. Was he feeling apologetic about that?

"I was thinking of maybe mixing their ashes together in the box. You know, to mingle them."

"I wonder if the box wouldn't be a little awkward for sprinkling—scattering," Caroline self-corrected. "They might all come tumbling out at once."

"I think we'll be able to scatter them better from the bags," I began.

"—and mingle them on the ground," Angie

finished. "But the bags are pretty thick plastic, and held together with a very strong staple. Maybe we could go to the hardware store and buy some scissors."

"Do you remember the silver lizard Mom had on top of the wooden box?"

I did. A silver lizard. Small. Dull silver. Given to her by Dad.

"Well. When I put both bags in the box, I threw in the lizard and its tail punctured a hole in Dad's bag, so I left it there," Jonathan paused, "you know, so the ashes wouldn't dribble out. So the lizard's tail is pretty sharp if we have a problem," he said, turning to Angie.

Jonathan looked at me.

"Why don't you scatter Dad's ashes and I'll do Mom's?"

"Perfect." I loved his taking charge and his strong desire to make this happen and happen well. More than anything, I wanted him to feel satisfied.

When the check arrived at the table, Jonathan took it, insisting, "Our treat."

Outside, Caroline and I stood together on the busy sidewalk in the cool, sunny day. The sky was a flawless blue, the play of warm sun and cool shadow in perfect balance. A day when the city looked cleansed. I looked at Caroline and felt my eyes fill with tears. For losses, I thought, past and to come.

I hadn't thought about my father, really thought about him, for a long time, and something was nudging me. We shared a father, Jonathan and I, the same man. But also not the same man. My father was the man I remembered from long, long ago in small moving images, hard to make out, rough, like a home movie. He was lean, young, with black curly hair, deep brown eyes, waving arms. He had a scary temper. He quoted poetry at dinner, sang songs from Gilbert and Sullivan, took me to Charlie Chaplin and Buster Keaton movies, which I didn't get, told funny stories like the one about the dog that ate all the pasta drying on a rack in his mother's kitchen. He took the stairs two at a time and beat out rhythms with his hands on the tops of tables. He read stories—acted them out in his great big voice. He was also the father who left, who was Tom's father, then Jonathan's.

Jonathan and Angie rejoined us and we started down Broadway.

"I think we should get some flowers," Angie said.

"What a good idea."

We approached a produce market in the next

block. An array of cylindrical pots full of flowers stood on the sidewalk behind protective plastic sheeting affixed to the awning over the sidewalk.

"What shall we get?"

"How about some of those mums." Angie pointed to bunches of spiky orange mums. "Nice and simple."

"And how about some cranberries," Caroline suggested as we entered the store, "to scatter."

Cranberries? Why cranberries? I did not ask.

Jonathan, in the open spirit of the day, took up her suggestion. "Let's see if they have some." They checked the shelves without finding any. Meanwhile Angie bought a fresh bunch of the mums.

At Eighty-Seventh Street, Jonathan suggested that we walk over to West End, continue down to Eighty-Fifth past their old building, and on to the park.

"Perfect," I said.

West End Avenue, a canyon of stone buildings adorned with burgundy, green, and gray awnings, was in bright shadow. I counted three buildings I had lived in at one time or another before I met Caroline and joined her in Connecticut. We passed the building where my mother had lived and died, the building where Tom and Myrna had lived after the divorce and before they moved out West. We passed the building where Dad and Barbara had lived for over thirty years. Everyone now was gone.

Caroline and I, strolling slowly, lagged behind.

"What was that about cranberries?"

"I don't know. Flowers, food. Christmas coming. A funny impulse. Don't laugh at me."

"I'm not laughing," I said, laughing. "Like the Egyptian pharaohs?"

"Something like that."

"You know, that conversation we had with them about Maggie? Whenever a conversation turns to spirituality—the mystery of life as Jonathan called it—my first thought is that I am not spiritual and I kind of back off in my mind. I don't know what people are talking about when they use words like 'transcendent' or 'spiritual.' I just don't relate to it. I think I've missed out entirely on this dimension of life."

"I don't think that's true," she said.

We walked along a row of brownstones, restored since I had lived in the neighborhood. Someone had placed red geraniums on the sills in the first-floor windows.

"The other day, when I was driving across the Connecticut River, I saw a big flock of birds in the sky just as they changed direction," I told her. "All of them together. And their dark wings suddenly, at the very same instant, flashed white. It was breathtaking and I had a feeling..."

"What sort of feeling?"

"A feeling of smallness, that there was nothing in the world but the immensity of those birds changing course in the sun, the beauty of it, the mystery, the miracle even, and of yourself, not looking at them, but actually being them. Them and you alive. It felt like a moment of eternity, however funny that sounds."

Caroline squeezed my hand. "Sounds pretty spiritual to me."

At Eighty-Fifth we turned west and stopped in front of number 350. Jonathan pointed out the living room and dining room windows on the fourth floor. Angie laid one orange mum on the smooth, gray stone step. We moved on toward Riverside Drive and entered the park.

We followed a path that led to the stone steps embedded in the huge outcropping of the island's bedrock, scoured four thousand years ago by an advancing glacier: Manhattan schist, its chips of mica sparkling in the sun. It rose up from the park, half buried in the debris left over from autumn: a mixture of green grass and taller, browning grasses. Dark, dried flowerheads danced above, and bare, gnarled trees clutched at the thin layer of soil over the rock.

From here we commanded several views: looking west, of the park falling gently toward the Hudson River, just now moving north with the incoming tide; looking south, of the big playground with its own smaller outcrop at one end; and looking east, at the street we'd just come from. People strolled the paths below. From the playground beyond we heard the shouts of children as they chased each other or bobbed up and down on seesaws, their mothers and fathers sitting on benches or pushing swings.

A man in a brown canvas jacket, balding and gray, stood at the edge of the grasses among some trees, his back to us. He seemed to be communing with his elderly dog, a golden retriever with white muzzle and contented face who lay in the sun.

We wouldn't be able to do anything while he was there.

"Go away," I whispered.

"He will, eventually," Caroline said. She wandered out onto the massive rock splayed out like a dark crust over the grassy rise.

"When he does," Jonathan said, "it'll just be us."

I wasn't the only one who'd been imagining that we'd have to sneak like thieves, perhaps stop and start at times, to accomplish our mission, that we'd be surrounded with people coming and going. But what we had was privacy, and a beautiful place exactly where Jonathan wanted it to be. A sunny day, warm for December, patterns of black branches against a blue sky.

"See that big rock down there by the playground?" I said. "You can barely make out the bronze plaque with the man's face on it. When I lived with Dad and Myrna, I used to bring Tom to the playground in his stroller when he wasn't much more than a toddler. Every time we passed that plaque, his hand would reach out toward the man's face. I'd stop and he'd say, in a kind of wonderment, 'Daddy.'"

The man and his dog moved off. We huddled. Jonathan opened the box. There, nestled inside, were the two bags of ashes, one of them pierced by the tail of the lizard. Each had a brass tag. Each closed with a metal twist tie.

Angie and Caroline stood back a little, Angie holding the bouquet of mums against her chest. Jonathan handed me Dad's ashes and he opened Barbara's. I felt compelled to go over the technique with him: hold the bottom of the bag up by one corner and hold the upper end of the opening a little lower, to get more control of the flow so the ashes wouldn't bunch up. Jonathan undoubtedly didn't need this instruction, but it made me feel better. He politely received my suggestions.

He pointed to a young tree partway down the hill. "How about around that tree?

"Perfect," I said.

And so, both following and leading each other, we stooped and waddled round and round the tree. We let our parents' ashes fall to the ground, intermixing them until there was nothing left in the bags and a path of lumpy, light gray ash circling the trunk, some of it already lifting in the breeze.

Acknowledgments

It has been a privilege to be a member of Carol Edelstein's Thursday Night Writers Workshop for the past thirteen years. I am grateful to the writers past and present who, under Carol's gentle and wise leadership, offer insight and motivation. Special thanks to Barbara Lucey and Ronnie Rom, whose early readings of some of these stories provided valuable feedback, and to Robin Barber, who, with Carol, makes Thursday evenings warm and engaging gatherings.

I am deeply indebted to Carol for her encouragement and insightful readings, re-readings, and suggestions. Without her editorial skills and generous gift of time, this book would still be a work in progress.

Thanks also to past and present members of the critique group hosted by Rita Bleiman, in particular Rita and Fred Contrada, Susanne Dunlap, Elaine Wolf, and Dee DeGeiso for helpful commentaries.

I am grateful to Judy Jablon and Pat Ruopp, who have offered invaluable insights and suggestions. Pat's willingness to read the whole manuscript was especially generous and helpful.

My warmest thanks to Fran Volkmann for her steady support, her astute comments on the manuscript, and her appreciation of these stories.

Special thanks to the Gallery of Readers Press and to Stephanie Gibbs for inviting my opinions and designing a beautiful book. And finally, thanks to Georgianne Nienaber for taking my picture.

About the Author

Joan Cenedella was born in Milford, Massachusetts, in 1936 and lived on Manhattan's Upper West Side from 1950 until she moved to Northampton, Massachusetts, in 1995. After graduating from City College in 1958, she worked at *Seventeen* magazine and Thomas Y. Crowell Publishers as a writer and editor. In 1970, she completed the master's degree program at Bank Street College of Education, and later earned her doctorate at Teachers College, Columbia University. During her tenure at Bank Street, from 1969 to 1995, she served in several roles: as teacher of children and graduate students, as Dean of Children's Programs, and as author of numerous writings on teaching and learning. She lives in Northampton with her partner, Fran Volkmann, and their dog Lucy.